WHO WANTS TO LOVE A BILLIONAIRE?

LAURA BURTON

BURTON & BURCHELL LTD

First Edition

Edited by R J Creamer

Written in U.S. English

 Created with Vellum

FROM THE BILLIONAIRES IN NEW
YORK SERIES

Who Wants to Love a Billionaire?

CHAPTER 1

THE QUIET SEAMSTRESS

J ulie yelped and sucked on her fingertip. A metallic taste flooded her mouth, and with a moan she jumped to her feet. She sped across the room to the kitchenette, then rummaged one-handed through the drawers.

The phone rang, prompting the cat to screech and bolt out of the room. Probably off to his favorite hiding place underneath the bed.

"Yes, yes, hello," Julie called out as she accepted the call. Her fingertip throbbed and she hissed against the pain as she sprayed the wound with antiseptic.

"Are you okay?" a worried voice crackled out of

the speaker. Julie fastened a Band-aid on her finger and took a breath.

"I'm fine, Emily, just pricked my finger again."

"Oh, that must mean you're making another dress."

Julie collapsed back into a chair at the dining table and made some adjustments to the controls on the sewing machine.

"Hmm," she said with a needle between her teeth. She finished fastening the last safety pin on the pink chiffon material and positioned it to sew. As she stepped on the pedal the needle bobbed up and down faster than a woodpecker hammering against a tree.

"Listen, I have a new client, and I think you're really going to like him," Emily's voice barked over the sound of the motor. Julie stopped and stared at the phone intently.

"I don't know...," she began, unsure.

Emily and Julie attended Oxford University together and had been roommates. When they graduated, Emily ventured out to New York while Julie spent a year in Paris, working for one of Estelle's fashion lines. After building a rapport with the high-maintenance models, she landed a role in the New York office.

Emily was her best—and only—friend in the city.

"I'm five minutes away from your place. Are you home?"

Julie considered the idea of concocting a lie: She was at an underground party across town, or maybe volunteering at a soup kitchen in the Bronx? But she knew Emily would see right through it. "I can pick up some food? What are you in the mood for?"

Julie thought about it. What mood was she in? The pain in her finger dulled and gave way to the ache in her temples, and the back of her neck was tight. She spent all day hunched over the sewing machine and forgot to eat. Her stomach growled.

"We can order takeout," she mused aloud, warming to the idea of a visit.

"Great, and I'll pick up some Cinnabons for dessert."

Julie rolled her eyes and ended the call. Emily was obsessed with cinnamon rolls. Perhaps they reminded her of home? Or maybe Emily just had a sweet tooth.

She flitted around the apartment in an attempt to tidy up. When the buzzer sounded, she scanned the room quickly before letting Emily in.

"Hey, girl." A plume of perfume covered Julie and caught in the back of her throat as Emily threw her arms around her.

"What are you doing tonight? I've got you a date."

"That fast? Emily, when I said, 'I don't know,' I didn't mean, 'go ahead.' I've got work to do."

Emily flicked back her sleek brown hair and raised

a hand. She was having none of it. That was Emily. Despite being nearly a foot shorter than Julie, she was the bossy one. And Julie often found it impossible to argue, once Emily had a plan in mind.

Julie glanced over at the half-made dress lying on the table and bit her lip. She had to finish it before the weekend was out, but the stiffness in her neck had her rolling her head side to side with a moan.

Emily placed a Cinnabon bag on the counter and strutted to the table.

"It's a beautiful day to fall in love, you know." Her false lashes fluttered, and she grinned at Julie, while resting her hip against the table.

"You don't still believe in that, do you?" Julie rooted through the Cinnabon bag and pulled out a roll. It was still warm.

Emily squared her shoulders and placed her slender hands on her hips.

"Well, I am a matchmaker. It would be terrible if I didn't believe it." Her voice was soft and musical—a stark contrast to Julie's deep voice.

Julie devoured the cinnamon roll and licked the frosting off her fingertips. *Emily has a point*, she thought.

"Well, I'll need your help. I have no idea what to wear, and you need to tell me about this guy. I hate blind dates."

Emily clapped her hands, her black and silver

painted nails sparkled in the setting sunlight as she offered a gleeful smile.

"Oh, don't you worry, I came prepared."

Emily left the apartment for a short while and returned with a mountain of shopping bags.

"He's a high-profile client, and we need you to look the part."

"You mean, less like a poor seamstress and more like a Hollywood actress?" Julie asked wryly.

"Exactly." Emily nodded as she pulled out a long maroon gown.

"I'm the woman in the red dress? How cliché." Julie walked over to inspect it. Boning to the bodice, refined darts from the waist to the bust. The skirt was heavy, perhaps weighted at the hemline. It was exquisite.

"I can't accept this." Julie looked up at Emily, who was brimming with pride. She knew she chose well.

"Of course, you can. How many dresses have you made for me over the years? I owe you."

She ushered Julie out of the room toward the bedroom and instructed her to try it on.

"So, what is he like?" Julie shouted through the closed door as Emily waited on the other side. She fiddled with the fastenings on the back of the gown and unzipped it.

"He's an introvert, like you," Emily replied, her

voice muffled. Julie undressed out of her sweat pants and shirt—the same clothes she had been wearing since Friday and stepped into the gown.

"Tall? Hair color? Eyes? Hobbies?"

"He's taller than me."

"Most people are—"

"Brown hair but sort of golden in the sunshine, dark brooding eyes."

Julie shrugged the sleeves up to her shoulders.

"Hmm. Keep talking."

"He's in the movie business."

Julie sucked the air in through her teeth with a hiss. She didn't like dating men like that.

"Don't you dare judge; he's a total sweetheart." Emily pushed open the door and gave Julie a reproachful look. Julie feigned horror and attempted to work the zipper, but her arms wouldn't bend that way. Emily tutted and walked over to her.

"Let me do it," she said as she yanked on the material, forcing Julie's posture to straighten.

"You need to stop hunching like that; it's bad for your spine."

Julie turned to look at Emily, who gasped and raised her hands to her mouth.

"You look breathtaking." Her eyes glistened.

Julie swallowed and looked back at herself, feeling self-conscious. Yes, she made extravagant dresses every day. But that was for high-end women, with enough class and demure to carry off the look. Julie was just... Julie. She preferred comfort over class, and the red designer dress did not accurately reflect her bank balance.

"Emily, don't you think this is mis-selling?"

Emily chuckled.

"Don't be ridiculous. You're not an insurance policy." She marched out of the room. "Take a shower, and I'll order us some food," she called back.

Julie sighed heavily, wondering what Emily had gotten her into. She was going on a date with a rich bachelor who probably dated Academy Award-winning actresses, and maybe even half of New York. But Emily did say he was an introvert and sweet. Perhaps he was the tortured, yet brilliant screen-writer who rubbed shoulders with high-profile people but didn't feel like he belonged in that world. *It's only one date,* Julie thought to herself as she prepared to take a shower. She grinned and stepped into the steam.

CHAPTER 2

THE SHY BILLIONAIRE

"I don't like this," Harry said as he straightened his tie, looking in the floor-length mirror.

"What's the matter, sir?" Benjamin said from the door; Harry's head of security and stood perfectly still.

Harry turned to him and anxiously patted his blonde wavy hair in a vain attempt to smooth it out.

"Why did you let me sign up for this? Matchmaking... what a joke." He stuffed his shirt into his pant trousers and looked wildly around the room.

"It's on the bed," Benjamin said calmly, knowing

exactly what Harry was looking for. Harry marched over to the bed and picked up his inhaler.

"Do you think it's too late to cancel? I could say I'm sick. Or kidnapped? Held at ransom?" He laughed derisively at his own words and waved his hands. "Don't answer that." He took his inhaler and breathed in slowly.

"I believe you will have fun. You always do," Benjamin said.

Harry paced the room and glanced at his watch. It was time to go. Snakes writhed within his gut and he dabbed the back of his neck with a towel.

"I'm a mess. Why do I agree to these stupid blind dates?"

"Because you're lonely, and if left to your own devices, you end up with the wrong person."

Harry shot Benjamin a hard look. He couldn't argue but did not appreciate his tone.

"Thanks for that," he said dismissively. Benjamin inclined his head. The phone rang, prompting Harry to turn hot on his heels and retrieve it from his nightstand.

"Harold, I need to know if you're going to be at the charity dinner this weekend."

"How many times... please don't call me that," Harry said. He hated his name. His schoolboy friends in England bullied him mercilessly for it. Since moving to New York, he was able to get away with just Harry, but certain individuals stuck with his Christian name.

"I'm your mother, you will always be Harold to me," the mature woman said firmly. "Now are you going to be there or not?"

"I'll be there." Harry sighed and tugged at his collar. His neck felt like it was being squeezed by the Armani shirt.

"Good. You'll be bringing a plus one, I assume? You know Ebony will be there...."

Harry swallowed. Ebony was his ex-fiancé. A feisty redhead who took an interest in the stock markets, and despite their engagement, ran off with Phillipe, her massage therapist. At first Harry thought she was going to those appointments because the stress of being in the pit was making her shoulders tight. Turns out, she was seeing him for more than a neck rub. Ebony broke Harry's heart and married Phillipe two years ago. They moved to Surrey, and word had it that they had a couple of dogs in their country home and enjoyed clay pigeon shooting on the weekend. It now sounded as though country life with her masseuse wasn't all grand.

"I'll have a plus one, and it will not be Ebony, Mother. I can't talk right now, I have a date."

"Oh? What is her name?" Harry's mother asked in a cheerful tone. Harry heard the slight skepticism in her voice that he was making it up.

"Julie," he replied faster than his brain could compute. It was the only name on his mind. The name of the woman he was going on a blind date with. He knew hardly anything about her. Emily, the match-maker, thought an air of mystery allowed for the date to feel less like a set-up and more like an organic meeting.

"Well, good for you. I assume I will meet her this weekend?" Harry's mother asked innocently. Harry swallowed.

"Yes, of course."

They exchanged their good-bye's and he ended the call. Harry looked up at Benjamin who had one eyebrow raised so high it almost disappeared into his dark hairline.

"Great, just when I think there couldn't be any more pressure to like this woman. Now I've got to persuade her to come with me to England this weekend."

"You might like to make a good first impression, then." Benjamin shifted his weight and opened the door for Harry. "Punctuality is always a good start."

Harry gasped at his watch and took a breath.

"Right, let's not waste any time," he said and marched out of the door.

CHAPTER 3

A Blind Date

Julie walked into the restaurant and looked around the tables, scanning the room for her date. Emily had not even shown her a picture of the man she was to meet, which sent her anxiety into overdrive.

"You want this to feel as natural as possible. No Facebook stalking. Get to know each other, the *real* way," Emily had said as she ushered her into the cab.

The restaurant was cozy, with low chandeliers and dark walls. A harpist played Chopin in the corner by a large pane window, and everyone spoke in dull tones.

The blonde hostess looked up from her stand and eyed Julie carefully.

"Do you have a reservation?"

"Sure, my name is Julie Andrews."

The hostess pursed her lips and surveyed the leather-bound book on the stand.

"I'm meeting Harold Jackson," Julie added quickly, noticing she was having difficulty finding her name. The hostess looked up and raised a hand to her collarbone.

"Oh, why didn't you say? This way—" She sauntered off with her head held high. Julie followed, holding her dress to keep from stepping on the material. She silently reprimanded herself for not adjusting the length, but Emily didn't exactly give her much time.

"Here we are. Mr. Jackson has not arrived yet." She gestured to a small table in a dark corner of the restaurant. Julie settled in one of the leather chairs and squinted at the menu. She could hardly make out the words in the dim light.

"Can I get you a drink?"

Julie looked up at the hostess. Her painted nails were drumming her hip bone, and Julie noticed that the hostess' smile did not reach her eyes.

"Um," Julie said as she glanced across the room. She caught sight of a man waiting by the front.

Is that him?

She blinked and looked back up at the hostess, who appeared to be having trouble resisting the urge to roll her eyes. Her brows twitched and she blinked hard as her smile grew wider.

"I'll give you a few minutes to think about it," she said, as if through gritted teeth. Off she went, leaving Julie alone in the dark. She shuffled around in her seat, smoothing out her dress. The lace overlay irritated the skin on her arms and collarbone; she wriggled her shoulders and arched her back. The boning offered very little movement, keeping her upright when she longed to relax her posture and sink back into the comfortable leather seat. The sound of footsteps caught her attention and she stopped fidgeting and looked up.

"Here you are, Mr. Jackson." The hostess' voice was sickly sweet now, and Julie noticed her eyes were sparkling.

"Thank you. Hello, Julie, I'm terribly sorry for being late—have I kept you waiting long?"

Julie rose from her seat and opened her mouth to speak but before she could say a word, the hostess jumped in.

"Oh no, no, not at all."

Julie closed her mouth again and shot a quizzical

look at her before refocusing in on the man standing with his hand held out. She took it.

"You're Harold?" she asked shyly her eyes lingering on his face. His hair was wavy and cut short at the sides, a rich golden shade, almost like caramel. He had the darkest eyes Julie had ever seen and his hand was softer than cashmere.

"Please," he began as they broke apart and took their seats. "Call me Harry." His voice was slightly husky, and he had a gentleness about him that set Julie at ease. They eyed each other for a few moments, completely forgetting about the hostess standing beside them.

"I'll send over a server shortly. In the meantime, if you need anything please just let one of the busboys know."

Harry pressed his index finger to his lips for a moment in thought, then scratched the back of his neck. "I do apologize for being a nuisance, but do you think we could sit somewhere else?" he asked.

Julie eyed the hostess carefully and apart from a slight nose flare, there was no sign of offence. Yet, Julie was certain that this woman did not want to find another table in the busy restaurant.

"I had assumed you wanted to be seated some-where quiet?" she began, a tinge of annoyance in her voice. Harry nodded.

"I wonder if your balcony is free?"

The hostess nodded slowly and closed her eyes for a long moment.

"If you just give us a few minutes, I'll have it ready for you shortly." She turned and left without so much as a glance in Julie's direction. Julie looked back at Harry and eyed the perfectly tailored suit he was wearing.

"I'm all right sitting here. We don't need to cause any trouble," she offered tentatively. Harry leaned forward and squinted at her.

"Yes, thing is… I can't see you. When Emily said this was a blind date, I didn't think it would be one of those… you know, blind dates."

"Where the lights are off?"

"That's it." Harry laughed. His hair was darker in the low lighting and his face was shadowed.

"You do look like a tall, dark, and handsome stranger though," Julie blurted out before her brain caught up. She gawped at Harry for a moment, realizing she said her thoughts aloud. To her delight though, he chuckled appreciatively.

"I didn't even know they had a balcony," Julie added, mostly to herself. Harry looked sheepish.

"I'm a friend of the owner," he said shyly. Julie cocked a brow.

"Of this restaurant? Or the entire Martinelli franchise?"

Harry clasped his hands together, interlocking his broad fingers and tilted his head side to side.

"Tommy and I went to Eton together." He shrugged lightly.

"Tommy… Martinelli?"

Harry nodded. Julie wanted to whistle and slump back into the chair, but her tightly fitted bodice held her in place.

"You mentioned Eaton… are you from England?" Julie asked, almost hopeful. It would be nice to meet another Brit in the city. Harry, however, shook his head.

"No, I was born in Idaho."

"Oh, don't tell me, your parents are potato farmers?" Julie asked without thinking. As soon as the words escaped her lips, blood rose to the surface of her cheeks.

That is so offensive, why did I say that?

"I'm so sorry, I didn't mean it to come out like that," she added quickly. Harry waved his hands.

"It's fine. I like your humor," he said lightly. "Yes, my father was a potato farmer. I have no idea why, but he loved his work," he explained.

The hostess reappeared before Julie could comment.

"Your table is ready, if you will follow me." She turned on her heels and walked slowly, while Julie scrambled to her feet. As if he possessed spider-senses, Harry lunged to her side and held out his hand just as Julie's ankle gave way. She cried out and grasped his arm as his grabbed her waist, pulling her upright again. For the briefest moment, the heat of Harry's hands warmed her back and she glanced into his beautiful eyes as she clutched his arm.

"Thank you, I'm so clumsy in heels," she said breathlessly as they broke apart and Julie regained balance. Harry's cheeks were flushed. The corners of his eyes creased as he flashed her a grin.

"I promise I'm not judging. I have no idea how anyone can walk in them." He held out his arm and Julie slid her hand to rest on the crook. They followed the hostess in silence, Julie grinning despite herself. Her heart was doing a tap dance and her ears were ringing.

Harry held open the glass door and Julie stepped out.

The black sky was dotted with twinkling stars and a small table sat in the middle of a little garden. Large palm trees and potted flowers surrounded them, and if it wasn't for the small iron fence behind the table, Julie would never have guessed they were on a balcony. Fairy lights glowed like candles all around and a single red rose stood proudly on the table. Julie took a seat and watched Harry take his. He looked out at the huge moon shining in the sky. Its mystical rays illuminated his face and the sight made Julie want to sigh.

He's so dreamy.

"You can see Central Park from here," he mused. He was right. The huge trees framed the view of the grass banks and Julie could just make out the horse-drawn carriages going up and down the paths.

"Good evening, I am Merlin and I'll be your server today," a deep voice rumbled at them. Julie jumped and looked back to see a tall African American man with broad shoulders and chocolate brown eyes. His head was totally bald, and he had a smooth accent.

"Merlin, is that your real name?" Harry asked. Merlin flashed his white teeth as he shifted his weight and raised his hands as if he was caught red-handed.

"Yes, sir. My mom was a big fan of the story," he said. "Bless her soul." He looked up at the heavens and kissed his fingertips.

"Me too, *Sword in the Stone*. My grandfather used to read it to me," Harry exclaimed. Julie clapped her hands with excitement.

"Me too. Well, I watched the movie almost every day of my childhood." She laughed. "At least, that's what my memory tells me."

The three of them smiled fondly for a moment,

reveling in the memory of their childhood, when Merlin snapped his fingers and broke the spell.

"Are you ready to order?"

"So then I was talking to this actor, who did not want to relocate to Vancouver, and I had to pull a lot of strings to keep filming in Toronto. But I did it."

Julie dabbed her mouth and picked up a glass as Harry smiled bashfully at her. "I'm boring you, aren't I? I'm so, sorry."

Julie swallowed her drink before shaking her head.

"Not at all. It's fascinating. So you're a movie producer?" She set her glass down and picked up her knife and fork. The steaming plate of food had her stomach rumbling. Harry spent the entire time talking about… everything. They jumped from movies, to New York traffic, to the matchmaking business, then onto pineapples, and he spent a considerable time telling stories about his work.

"Yes, it's the best job in the world," Harry said, smiling broadly. His cheeks were flushed and the speed he was talking had Julie wondering if he was nervous.

"Doesn't it make you the boss? You know, if you're

the producer?" Julie asked. Harry rubbed the back of his neck and gave her an awkward look.

"I guess...."

"Why didn't you move the set to Vancouver, then?"

Harry pointed at her before wiping the perspirant from his brow.

"You're not the first person to ask me that. But this actor was the star of the show, if he left it would kill ratings."

"Hmm." Julie glanced out at Central Park in thought. "So, you're the boss, but you have to keep the star actors happy." She looked back at Harry who was nodding as he chewed.

"Hit the nail on the head, yes."

He was so agreeable, Julie noticed. He was charming, yet adorably bashful. Not the typical alpha male she had expected to meet and nothing like her previous boyfriends.

"I'd love to know more about you. I'm sorry I've been talking about me a lot. I ramble when I'm nervous. Not that you're making me nervous, you're wonderful." Harry stopped talking and took a breath. His uncertainty was endearing; Julie imagined he must have a whole team around him to stop everyone from taking advantage of him.

"I'm a seamstress. I make clothes for Estelle's fashion line," she offered, eyeing his reaction. Usually she received a shrug or a faint smile in return from her dates. Being a seamstress was not considered a glamorous job in the city. Men typically preferred to date the models wearing her dresses.

Harry's brows raised so high it made his eyes look huge. Like two dark saucers shining in the moonlight.

"That's remarkable," he said. There was no sign of sarcasm. He genuinely appeared impressed. Pride rose from Julie's stomach and she beamed at his response. "You must be the best seamstress in the country. I've heard of Estelle, and she's very picky."

"Thank you," Julie said, surprised at his words. She never felt so validated. "I love it. I mean, I constantly have a sore neck and back from hunching over my machine all day, every day, but I wouldn't change that for a boring nine-to-five."

"I can give great massages," Harry said a little too fast. Realization dawned on his face. "I didn't mean— oh boy. Forget I said that. I was just thinking aloud."

It was too late, though. Julie's mind had already raced ahead. She imagined his broad hands rubbing her back and all the tight muscles melting under his touch. She inadvertently moaned.

"No, that's amazing to know." She closed her eyes, lost in the vision. Harry cleared his throat, bringing Julie back to her senses. She covered her mouth with her hands and laughed. A casual smirk crossed his face.

From that moment on, the two of them relaxed and enjoyed their food while admiring the beautiful setting. The traffic sounds from below served as the only reminder that they were in New York, and not in a magical fairy garden. They finished their food and just gazed at each other for a long moment. This time, neither of them were blushing.

"I've really enjoyed spending time with you," Harry said, his voice deep and sure. Julie bit against her growing smile.

"Me too" was all she could say. The attraction between them was tangible in the air. It swirled around them and warmed places in Julie's body that she didn't expect. Like the hollow of her neck, the curve of her spine. She swallowed against the dryness in her mouth.

Harry leaned forward and gently took her hands in his. Julie's heart fluttered in response.

"Would it be too presumptuous of me to assume we will have a second date?" he asked, a bit of an Eaton accent coming through. Julie had never heard anyone speak to her in such a formal way, except for the private-school boys back in England. She nodded shyly. "I have to go to a charity event this weekend." He took a nervous breath and squeezed Julie's hands. "I would love to take you as my plus one."

His words sank like rocks in the pit of Julie's stomach. Sitting in this tight gown for a few hours was torture enough. The idea of attending some fancy charity dinner with cameras, other famous people and all that came with those kinds of affairs had Julie's stomach doing backflips. She did not like attention. Couldn't they just hang out at her apartment and watch Netflix like normal people? As she prepared to turn him down, the hopeful look on Harry's face melted her resolve.

"Okay, but can we do something else first?"

Harry let go of her hands and sat back with his brows raised again. "What did you have in mind?"

CHAPTER 4

An Ugly Surprise

"I have to admit, I've never done this before," Harry said warily as he helped Julie scale the steps into the carriage. He glanced across the road to Benjamin, who was standing in the shadows and gave him a nod. He craned his neck to look back to see the rest of the security team in position. They were perfectly safe, but it was not advisable for a billionaire to take a nighttime stroll through Central Park. At least they were in a carriage.

"Neither have I," Julie said. "It's such a beautiful night though, don't you think it'll be lovely?" She settled down on the wooden bench. Harry climbed up into the carriage and gave her a sheepish grin in response. He pulled out a red rose from his jacket and handed it to her.

"A red rose, for the damsel in the red dress," he said as he gave her his best smolder. "I stole that from a movie."

"Did you take this from the restaurant?" Julie asked pointedly.

Harry's smile faltered, a little deflated by her reaction.

Clearly this woman misses nothing.

Despite her disapproval, she hesitantly took the flower. "And I suppose you plan to steal my heart, too?" she asked coyly. Her eyes glowed like lamps, and her lips were round and plump. Sitting in such close proximity sent rushes of heat through all parts of Harry's body. He swallowed nervously.

"I—" His voice was too high. He swallowed harder and cleared his throat. "I wouldn't dream of it."

Julie turned away and looked down.

"Oh" was all she said. The carriage rolled forward and the steady sound of the horses' hooves hitting the path was relaxing. Harry rubbed his sweaty palms against his pant legs.

You can do this, Harry. Be cool.

He softly pulled back Julie's white blonde hair from her neck and she turned to look at him. Their noses hovered less than two inches apart. Her uneven breaths tickled his cheeks.

"I only mean, I would never assume your heart was for anyone to own," he said quietly. She blinked her long lashes and her lips fell apart slightly. "But if it was… then it must be earned. Not taken." He spoke barely above a whisper. She stared at him for a moment, then he heard her breath catch and saw her pupils dilate. Her plump lips curved upward and her eyes sparkled.

Nice save.

The wheels of the carriage bumped, and Julie cried out as she fell forward. Harry instinctively held her up. Had he not reached out, she would have face-planted in his lap. He inwardly laughed at the thought.

"Are you all right?" he asked as she righted herself, her hand pressed against her heaving chest.

"Yes, I'm fine," she replied, a little breathless. "That just caught me off guard."

"Are you always this clumsy?"

Julie glared at him and a look of defiance rose in her face. She gestured to her dress.

"It's this stupid gown," she said. "I can hardly breathe, let alone move properly. I'll have you know that when I'm wearing normal clothes, I'm not clumsy at all."

Harry gave her a casual smirk.

LAURA BURTON

"Oh really? You sure about that?" he asked, pointing to the Band-aid on Julie's finger. She followed his line of sight and smiled bashfully. Sensing she was a little distracted, Harry moved closer and took her hand. He raised it to his face and gently pressed his lips on her finger. "Well, I'm sorry you don't feel comfortable. For what it's worth... you look like a million dollars."

It was true. Her milky complexion was a stark contrast to the deep shade of red she was wearing, and the dress fit her like a glove, accentuating her curves and flowing out at the bottom. Her blonde hair hung in loose waves over her shoulders and her big eyes had him captivated all evening. What color were they? Amber? Yellow? Brown? Sometimes all three. They kept changing. Like being drawn to a magnet, he moved forward and stopped barely an inch away from her lips. He waited. Her eyes were studying him and he could see her mind racing, trying to decide what to do. Then the carriage jolted, and their lips collided. Harry cupped her face with his hands and moved tenderly. Julie moaned or sighed; he wasn't sure. Her small hands clutched the back of his jacket, bidding him to continue. Fireworks set off in all directions in Harry's brain. His lips tingled and he felt it all the way down his arms to his fingertips. The kiss ended too soon, and Julie moved back a little leaving Harry wanting more.

"I'm sorry," Harry said quickly. Tightness spread across his chest and he padded his jacket looking for the familiar shape of his inhaler. He felt it pressed up against his shirt.

"For what?" Julie asked.

"For the pun."

"What pun?"

Harry pulled out the inhaler and turned away quickly as he took a deep breath.

"Are you okay?" Julie asked.

He calmed. Turned back to her and held up the inhaler with a broad grin.

"You take my breath away."

Harry clasped his hands behind his back as he strolled beside Julie along the road. Benjamin and his team were close by but keeping a distance, in the hope Julie wouldn't notice. He did not want to suffocate her with all the security on their first date, or deal with all the questions that inevitably came with finding out he had an entourage.

"Well, this is me," Julie announced as they came to a stop. Harry looked up at the steps to a multi-story apartment building.

"You have a green door," Harry thought aloud. Julie looked up at it.

"Yes, I do."

Harry gritted his teeth.

Why did I say that?

Nerves were kicking in again.

"Green is my favorite color, so I'll remember that."

"You'll... remember the color of my door?" Julie's puzzled look sent blood rushing to the surface of Harry's skin. He was certain his entire face must look beetroot red now.

"I don't know why I said that, I don't mean to sound—"

"—like a stalker?" Julie asked. Harry stopped breathing for a moment and stared at her in horror. Julie's face broke out into a wicked smile and she brushed his arm with her fingers.

"You're lucky I find it endearing and not creepy."

Harry gulped. What now? Do they hug and say good-bye? Could he lean in for another kiss? Maybe he should shake her hand. While he stood there, his brain running through the scenarios, Julie rose on tiptoes and gently brushed her lips against his cheek.

"I've had a wonderful evening," she said. The warmth in her voice made Harry feel fuzzy and happy inside. He nodded, unable to find his voice. Julie eyed him carefully, her head tilted to one side. She turned away, then shot him one more look.

"You know, you're a bit different. But you really are a gentleman," she said. Harry could detect a hint of surprise in the tone of her voice. He swallowed and raised his hand in an awkward wave.

"That's me." He flashed her a Cheshire cat smile. Julie shook her head to herself and picked up her dress as she climbed the steps.

"I had a wonderful time too," Harry called after her. "I think you're great. Better than great. I'm sorry I'm weird. But I'd like to see you again!" Sweat started to form above his lip and across his brow.

Stop talking. Stop talking.

"You *will* see me again. We're going to that charity event, remember?" Julie called back, now fiddling with her keys. She stood at the top of the steps in the elegant gown, and her long blonde hair flowed freely to her lower back. She looked like a goddess.

"The charity thing...," Harry murmured to himself. His mother's face popped into his head and he jumped with realization. "Oh yes, the charity thing. I'll call you about it tomorrow?" He shouted. Julie nodded back at him as the door swung open.

"Good night, Harry."

He raised a hand to his heart as it fluttered with excitement at the sound of his name.

"Good night."

~

Harry returned to his apartment in a haze. He paid no attention to the muttering staff grouped together across the street. He did not hear Benjamin speaking to him in urgent tones as they sat in the back of the car. He was not even aware of the engine rumbling and the car swinging side to side as the driver navigated the roads. He just sat in a bubble of happiness, replaying the events of the evening.

Julie twirling her platinum hair and blinking at him coyly across the dinner table at the restaurant and the way she gazed at all of the lights in their private balcony and took in the view. She scrunched up her nose and wriggled it to the side at one point, as if trying to scratch an itch without using her hands. And she sat so poised and elegant, though a hint of a pout told him that perhaps she would prefer to be wearing something more relaxed.

"It's this silly dress, you see."

He couldn't remember the exact words she used, but Harry found it refreshing that Julie was so honest. In the Hollywood business, women rarely said a word about their clothes in a negative way. All the actresses walked in the most impractical shoes and dangerously tight and revealing gowns. Harry often wondered if there was some unspoken competition between the women: Who wore it better, whose heels were highest, how many ruffles could they fit on a skirt?

"Sir, I need you to listen."

Harry blinked out of his daze and looked at Benjamin.

"Sorry, I was miles away…."

"Yes. I need to make you aware of an event."

"What is it? Pushy paparazzi? Rogue reporters?"

"This is no laughing matter, sir."

"Sorry, Benjamin."

"It has been brought to my attention that you were being followed."

"By who?"

"It is uncertain at this stage, and we were able to deter the individual from coming too close."

"Who do you think they are? Surely you have your theories."

"If I'm honest, I think it was a hired investigator."

Harry stared at Benjamin's bushy brows with intensity as he tried to process the news. He puffed out the air from his cheeks as the car came to a stop.

"Right, well thank you for informing me." Harry made to leave the car.

"That's not all."

He stopped short and looked pointedly at Benjamin, whose face had turned grim. He slowly pulled out a crumpled piece of paper from his jacket.

"One of my men found this. It's addressed to you."

Harry took the note and smoothed out the creases to read the single line.

Walk away now, or I will destroy you.

CHAPTER 5

LADY LUCK

J ulie closed the door and twirled on the spot with a squeal.

"So, how did it go?"

She jumped and cried out in surprise at the unexpected voice, then turned to see Emily sitting cross-legged on the couch. A black cat purred in her lap, and she looked up at Julie as she walked in.

"Emily. What are you still doing here?" she asked. Emily raised a tub of Ben & Jerry's and gave a happy smile.

"I couldn't leave Tabby here all alone," she cooed as she tickled the cat's ears. Tabby purred and looked at Julie as if to say, "I like her more than you." Julie stood rooted on the spot, still reeling from shock. Then, a rush of excited energy flooded her veins and she broke into a dance.

"It was amazing," she said breathlessly. Emily moved the cat and jumped to her feet with a little scream.

"Tell me everything. Spare no details."

"Harry is so sweet, and he's totally not what I expected," Julie began, her eyes glazing over as she replayed the date.

"Oh, *Harry*, is it? You're on informal terms, then?"

"We had our own private balcony with fairy lights and everything."

"How romantic." Emily sighed and clasped her hands together.

"He kept apologizing for things," Julie noted. "Oh, I nearly forgot." She raised a hand to her cheek with horror. Emily rested her hands on her hips and surveyed Julie.

"What?"

Julie looked at Emily as if she was seeing her for the first time. "I was so clumsy, like the stereotypical girl in a romcom. It was mortifying." She arched her back and attempted to reach the zipper, but Emily marched across the room and took over.

"So, are we talking, you dropped your purse on the

floor? Or you spilled your drink over the table?" She loosened the gown and Julie could breathe deeply for the first time in hours.

"I nearly fell flat on my face," she said pointing to the long skirt of her gown. She picked up the dress and tiptoed to her bedroom. Emily followed closely behind.

"Nearly? So, you just tripped, right?"

Julie grinned as she recalled Harry holding her tightly; she could still feel the warmth of his hands on her back when she thought about it.

"Harry caught me."

Emily nodded with approval.

"I knew it. I just knew you two would get along."

Get along? He's perfect.

"So, he's a client of yours, right? What is he looking for?"

"A kitchen broom."

"Huh?"

"Don't be daft, Julie. He is looking for a girlfriend, *obviously*." Emily rolled her eyes with a tut. "And after meeting him, your face came to me."

Julie shrugged the dress off her shoulders, stepped out of it and carefully draped it over a chair. Then she grabbed a pair of leggings from her dresser and yanked them on. The soft stretch material felt like coming home after a long day.

"He kissed me."

"Of course, he did," Emily replied, nodding with approval. "How was it? Were there fireworks?"

"Definitely."

"Are you going to see him again?"

"He's going to call me tomorrow, but he already said he wanted me to be his plus one at a charity thing."

Emily paced the room in thought.

"Charity thing," she said to herself. "Hmm. I wonder which one he's talking about. We're going to need to take you shopping again."

Julie pulled on a sweater and collapsed onto her king-size bed, exhaling deeply. Tabby meowed to announce his arrival and leapt onto Julie's legs and stretched out. Julie tickled his tummy.

"Okay, you've given me the highlights. Now tell me everything. Start from the beginning and leave nothing out." Emily climbed onto the bed as well, and sat up like an excitable puppy, waiting for a treat. Match-making was Emily's job and her bright, expectant eyes showed Julie that this was the part she loved most, so she told her everything. Even the short conversation they had with Merlin and their shared favorite story, *The Sword in the Stone*. She described the carriage ride. The kiss. Harry's lame joke after it. Everything.

"… and then I came in and you nearly scared me to death," Julie finished.

Emily's eyes were tearing up.

"I told you," she said, obviously pleased with herself. Julie fell back onto the plush pillows and stretched her arms out with a yawn. They had been talking for hours. It had been a long day hunched over the sewing machine, followed by a date strapped into a restrictive dress; the muscles in Julie's back screamed at her.

"Told me what?"

Emily propped herself up on an elbow and looked pointedly at Julie.

"I told you it was the perfect day to fall in love."

Julie threw a pillow at Emily's smug face.

"I'm not in love."

Yet, she thought silently.

J ulie woke up to the sound of dry heaving. She blinked into the sunshine to see Tabby's face towering over her and before she could move, the cat coughed up a sticky fur ball that fell right onto Julie's forehead.

"Gross," she moaned as she grabbed a tissue to wipe it away, then jumped out of bed. She was at the sink when the phone vibrated loudly on her nightstand. Tabby screeched at the noise and fled the room. Julie's heart thumped against her ribcage as she wiped her face with a towel and hurried to retrieve the phone.

"Hello?" she said in a high voice. She cleared her throat and tried to steady her nerves.

"Is this Julie Andrews?"

"Yes, yes this is she." Julie glanced at the number on her phone. The male's voice did not sound like Harry.

"Our client came in to collect her gown this morning. Problem is, the gown is not here. Please tell me you have it."

Julie's stomach lurched. In all of the excitement, she completely forgot about the dress she was working on. She glanced at the clock, her throat swelling up with anxiety.

"Yes, sorry, Frank. I brought it home to finish over the weekend."

"Julie, the client is coming back at 4 p.m. You better have it here, in perfect condition—don't forget it's not insured outside the office. If anything happens—"

"Nothing will happen. I'm just doing some final touches and will get a cab. I promise."

"Don't mess this up for me. You've already made me look like a fool once today."

Julie apologized again and hung up the phone. Frank worked with Julie at Estelle's fashion department. He was head of the department, but he acted like he was a king. There were three rules in the office: 1. No jokes. 2. No talking back to him and 3. No one taking work home. Julie snuck the dress out of the office to get away from the constant noise and bustle. There must have been over one-hundred sewing machines, almost always on the go, and the tension in the air quashed Julie's creativity. How could she focus with Frank breathing down her neck?

Estelle's fashion line took pride in having their own in-house dress-making department, but the way the workers were treated made Julie feel like she was working in a sweatshop. If it wasn't for Emily and her cinnamon rolls, Julie would have left New York a long time ago. Emily worshipped Estelle and thought Julie had the most glamorous job in the world; she didn't have the heart to explain just how unglamorous her job really was.

Julie was so busy frantically working on the dress that she did not notice her phone, which remained quiet all morning. If she had not been so caught up in the stress of getting her work done, she would have been on edge expecting Harry's call.

"You're cutting it close." Frank looked up from his watch and his eyes narrowed at Julie as she walked in. "Is it finished?"

Before Julie could respond, a tall slender woman

with her hair cut into a neat bob exploded into the room.

"Frank, darling, I need those dresses." Her high-pitched voice grated on Julie's ears and she internally winced as the woman barged past her. Julie hung up the dress and stood lamely by the desk, not sure whether to leave the room or speak up. It was Frank who dealt with the clients. Julie shouldn't even be in his office.

"Noelle, have I ever let you down?" Frank held out his hand and took the woman's hand in his, pressing his lips to her bony fingers.

"Hmm. There's a first for everything." She wiped her knuckles on her white pencil skirt and turned to the clothes rack sitting proudly in the center of the room.

Julie shot a nervous glance to Frank, who stood immobile as Noelle rummaged through the dresses like a bargain hunter as she made various noises of approval.

Noelle Sunderland was a formidable woman. She was one of Estelle's most senior managers. Always scrupulously dressed with only the latest trends, she kept her figure to an eye-wateringly tiny size. She walked and talked as if she were Estelle Voir, herself. Julie wondered if the harsh exterior was a mandatory requirement to be at her senior level in the company.

Are women only to be taken seriously when they walk around barking at people, treating the staff as peasants?

"Phil," Noelle shouted, snapping Julie out of her thoughts. The door swung open and a tall, balding man wearing tiny black spectacles hurried into the room. He glanced at Julie and they shared a mutual eye roll.

"Get these downstairs," Noelle snapped. Phil muttered something inaudible and wrestled with the clothes rack as he vacated the room. "Heaven's sake… careful!" Noelle shot a steely look at Frank. "The photoshoot was delayed by an hour. You were lucky the model was late, otherwise I would be speaking to HR and having your head."

Julie gasped, alerting Noelle of her presence. Noelle's eyes darted across the room and she studied Julie for a moment.

"And you are?"

"No one, she's nobody," Frank said quickly. Julie stared at him affronted.

"I'm Julie Andrews. I made those gowns."

"You're a seamstress?" The hint of disdain in her voice made Julie's blood boil. She offered a forced smile and a nod as Noelle tilted her head to the side as if weighing Julie up.

"You'll do." She turned back to Frank. "I'm taking

43

her with me for the afternoon. You don't mind, do you?"

Frank's mouth hung open so wide, Julie saw every single one of his veneers. Noelle, however, did not wait for a response. "Come," she barked and patted her thigh as if to summon a dog. As Julie followed, she glanced back at Frank who stood still, his face entirely red and his mouth opening and closing like a fish gasping its last breath.

CHAPTER 6

An Unexpected Greeting

"**D**id you find anything?" Harry asked Benjamin as he greeted him by the car. They walked together as a rally of paparazzi swarmed them. Benjamin shook his head before he gestured for the rest of the security team to step in and manage the chaos. The team stood like guards and forced the people back to create a clear path to the doors of Estelle's offices.

Paparazzi were like a different breed of humans. With no regard for personal space, they fought tooth and nail to get the best shot. Harry was used to it. His popularity soared three years ago when one of his movies broke box office records. It was a two-hour long space opera movie, with only one actor. Bradley Stokes. The whole shoot took less than six weeks and post production went surprisingly well. It was the least expensive movie he'd ever made, and it went viral.

Harry had many enemies. Which was odd, because he considered himself friendly and agreeable. But that was show business. It wasn't personal.

He wondered why anyone would care about him dating Julie. She was a seamstress. *What's the big deal?* Maybe the note he'd received the night before came from a disgruntled actor who didn't make the cut, or perhaps Julie had an ex-boyfriend who couldn't let her go? What did "Walk away now" really mean? Walk away from Julie or the current movie deal?

Harry shook his head and emptied his mind of his negative thoughts. He was scheduled to drop in on a promotional photoshoot for his upcoming release—a romance set in Ancient Greece, loosely based on Helen of Troy, the woman said to be so beautiful her face launched a thousand ships.

Julie's face could do that, Harry thought to himself. His heart warmed at the memory of her pout as she blinked at him, fluttering her lashes. The warmth spread from his chest throughout the rest of his body and he became weak at the knees.

"Harold, we were not expecting to see you." A tall

lady with an austere expression held out her thin hand for him to take.

"I'm just checking in, Noelle, don't worry. I'm sure you've got everything under control."

Harry glanced at the set. A massive green-screen filled the back of the hall, and two people posed for the photographer. A team dressed in black were positioning huge spotlights and a woman was crouched down to adjust the dress on one of the models. Harry looked back at Noelle, then tuned back in.

"Sabrina is sick. No matter, I have a stand-in and Bertie will photoshop Sabrina's head onto the stand-in's body." Noelle sounded bored; her eyes were drooping, and she stood resting her elbow in her hand and stroked a tuft of hair behind her ear. Harry turned and noticed the woman adjusting the model's dress had moved. His mouth fell open.

It's her.

She stood with her back arched and her right arm draped over the shoulder of Matt, the main character. He grasped the back of her gown roughly and her head went back, her long platinum hair flowing to her waist. Harry's stomach tangled as he swallowed against the dryness in his mouth.

"Kiss her cheek," Noelle, coming back to life, barked as she strutted across the hall to stand next to the photographer. Harry watched Julie flinch as Matt lowered his head to brush his lips against her cheek-bone. Harry's hands were balled into tight fists as he looked on. Julie's eyes flitted to him and widened as a look of recognition flashed across her face. Harry gave an awkward wave before he lowered his hand and stood rooted on the spot.

Max, the photographer, was the best of the best. Fast, to-the-point and very precise, he did not need much time to get the shots they needed, and within half an hour the entire shoot was finished. Matt dropped his hands and marched off without a word to Julie, who stood with her arms hanging by her sides and looking at Noelle for further instructions.

She wore a long Grecian gown. It was sheer and if it weren't for the modesty slip, there would be little left to the imagination. The way the dress draped over her body was so delicate and elegant, it gave Harry goose bumps. He found himself staring at Julie, who was looking so lost. He wanted to scoop her up in his arms and carry her out of the hall, away from all these people. This was not her world. She was so sweet, so tender, so beautiful; it seemed a crime to expose her to this environment.

Hollywood is brutal. Why did Noelle drag her into this?

Noelle barked instructions to her as if she were a dog. Not the gorgeous, respectable woman she was. But that was Noelle being Noelle; she treated everyone like that. She was known as the "battle axe," but she got things done. And that made her the best in the business.

Julie picked up the skirt of her dress and tiptoed bare foot across the hall. This was Harry's chance. But something held him back. The words of that note burned across his mind.

... or I will destroy you.

If the note is about her, is she worth the drama? In the face of adversity, Harry often ran as far as possible in the other direction. The media made him out to be a brooding, heartbreaker, who had little regard for anyone's feelings. He got the job done—much like Noelle. Only, he was not like Noelle, and his team orchestrated circumstances to make him appear "hardier" than he was.

Harry blinked out of his thoughts and noticed Julie approaching him. A waft of perfume filled his nostrils and her smile melted his resolve. How could he stop seeing her? That smile. He got a rush of dopamine every time he saw it.

"Hi there," Julie said, rubbing her arms.

"You don't speak to anyone! Don't forget your place, seamstress," Noelle yelled across the set. Harry's heart sank at her words.

Does she really have to be that harsh?

"It's all right Noelle, we're... friends."

Noelle's eyes narrowed as she looked from Harry to Julie, then returned her judging gaze to Harry. Huffing out a sigh of disgust, she marched off tutting to herself.

"I'm told you saved the day," Harry said mildly. Julie's face lit up at his words. She placed her hands on her waist and squared her shoulders.

"Oh sure, that's me. Always happy to save a photo-shoot from disaster." She laughed to herself. Harry tried not to glance down at her chest as it heaved up and down in that decadent dress. Her body moved fluidly and in a way that had him enchanted.

"I'm sorry I didn't call you this morning." Harry chewed the inside of his cheek and awkwardly scratched the back of his neck, thinking of a plausible lie to tell her. Should he let her know about the threat he received? Maybe she had an idea who wrote it?

"Oh, I didn't even notice."

Julie's words stung, as if a poisonous dart shot him right between the eyes. His face must have mirrored his feelings, because a look of horror crossed Julie's. "I'm so sorry. I didn't mean that to sound so...." She pushed her wavy hair back from her shoulders and sighed. "It's been a weird morning." She reached out and touched Harry's forearm briefly. Her fingers set off a chain reaction through his whole body.

"I see that. So modeling isn't your usual thing?"

Julie shook her head and nervously eyed someone

behind Harry before she could reply. The fast approaching footsteps alerted him to turn around.

"We have a situation with Matt," Benjamin muttered. Harry followed his line of sight to see Matt had returned and was looking at him intently, his broad arms folded making his shoulders look even bigger.

"I'm sorry," he said turning back to Julie. She eyed him expectantly, her hands still resting on her hips. "Are you free right now?"

Julie glanced back at Noelle who was standing off to the side, talking to the photographer, then she looked back at Harry, her eyes bright.

"I think so." It was a simple answer yet seemed to set off fireworks inside Harry's head.

"Great. I will come and find you in a minute."

Julie nodded coyly and walked toward Noelle but stopped and glanced back at Harry. They shared a mutual look of admiration and Harry's heart raced.

Taking a deep breath, he turned back toward Matt.

"Right. Let's see what he wants now."

CHAPTER 7

A Touch of Love

Julie maintained composure until she entered the changing room; she clenched her fists and did a little dance. Having only worked in the manufacturing side of the building, she hadn't had an opportunity to see the studio downstairs. The grandeur of the high ceilings and fancy equipment blew her away. Massive green-screens, tall, high-tech lighting equipment, and racks and racks of clothes. Oddly, the team of stylists that had been perfecting her hair and correcting the way her dress draped on the floor had Julie feeling giddy. The flashing lights and all eyes on her would usually be the idea of a nightmare, yet something about putting on that Grecian gown, wearing masses of blonde hair extensions, and layers of makeup made her feel like she was totally in character.

For a short time, she was in somebody else's shoes. Not the shy, simple seamstress living in a foreign country, but a gorgeous actress, modeling for the front cover of her next big Hollywood blockbuster.

She caught a glimpse of herself in the tall mirror and her heart skipped a beat. The hair and makeup team had transformed her to look like Helen of Troy. According to Greek myth, she was married when Paris—a prince from another land—instantly fell in love with her beauty. He launched an attack on Sparta to kidnap Helen.

How fitting to be in the arms of Matt Broker when Harry walked in; he was the last person she expected to see. Noelle told her nothing about the producers for the movie, only that she needed to stand-in for an actress who fell sick.

This day was turning out crazier than she could have dreamed. Emily would love this. It was a perfect opportunity to spend more time with Harry. Part of her wondered if Emily had somehow engineered it all; it wouldn't be surprising if her friend had something to do with the actress' mysterious illness. She'd known

Emily to take her matchmaking business far too seriously on occasion.

Julie stepped out of her dress and carefully draped it over the chair. She stared at it for a few moments deep in thought. A scenario played out in her mind of her wearing the dress and walking arm in arm with Harry in a beautiful garden, when a knock on the door snapped her out of her reverie. In a flash, she grabbed the dress back up and held it to her body like a shield.

"Yes," Julie called out in a startled tone. The door swung open and Julie yelped at the sight of Harry standing in the doorway while she stood there undressed.

"Sorry, I thought you meant I could come in." Harry's face turned crimson as he backed out of the room and quickly closed the door. Julie scrambled to pull on her jeans, jumping up and down to force the denim over her hips.

"I thought you were Noelle!" Bending down she picked up her rumpled shirt off the floor, stuffed it over her head, then smoothed the material over her stomach. "Okay"—she flicked her hair back and opened the door slowly—"you can come in."

Harry ruffled his hair and offered a sheepish smile.

"Hi," he said in a low, silky voice, as if they were meeting each other for the very first time. His bashfulness sent rushes of energy through Julie's body, wanting her to run over and throw her arms around his shoulders. She cleared her throat and forced herself to stop fantasizing.

"Hi," she said, trying to sound nonchalant.

The two of them stood facing each other, looking a little lost for a moment. They cast their eyes about the room as if waiting for further instructions. Julie surveyed him closely. His shirt revealed just enough of his collarbone to show off his tanned skin. As she scrutinized him, he brought his finger to his lips, and her eye caught the leather bracelet wrapped around his right wrist. He opened his mouth to speak, but seemed to change his mind.

Julie decided to break the tension. "So, where are we going?" The question snapped Harry out of a daze.

"Right. About that." He glanced behind him as if to check no one was eavesdropping, before he stepped inside and closed the door behind him. Julie took an automatic step backward; the two of them alone in the changing room sent flurries of excitement through her.

"Matt—you know the guy you were taking photos with—has a few concerns about the press tour, so I need to take a rain check."

"Oh" was all Julie could say, wishing she was more eloquent, or could at least muster up a few syllables.

"I'm really sorry." He shifted his weight uncomfortably and clapped his hands. "Are you free tonight?"

Julie was free. Her next batch of dresses were not due for another week, and besides work she had zero social life. When she wasn't working her fingers to the bone, her evenings consisted of Netflix marathons while snuggled up with Tabby. It was not the thing she needed to confess to the big-shot movie producer who was currently canceling their impromptu date.

"I'll have to check my diary," she joked, resisting the urge to laugh at herself. She decided to trust he wouldn't cancel again the next time one of the actors had a pressing need.

Harry nodded but his brooding manner sent Julie's thoughts back to the carriage ride through Central Park.

His furrowed brows and deep, piercing eyes were enough to lower any woman's defenses. Julie took a tentative step forward and touched his arm, realizing he didn't get her humor. A spark lit up behind his eyes at her touch. "I'm kidding. What did you want to do?"

CHAPTER 8

MUSIC FOR THE SOUL

Harry anxiously shifted in his seat in his office listening to Matt ranting about his costar Sabrina.

"I'm not doing the tour without her. You're going to have to sort it out."

"She's sick. What am I supposed to do?"

Matt shrugged and folded his arms. "Not my problem." He reclined against the back of his chair and eyed Harry shrewdly.

He thinks he owns me.

Harry wanted to take him by the scruff of the neck and demand more respect. His brother Jonas wouldn't even hesitate, but he owned a chain of CrossFit gyms and had the biceps to match the image. One punch would knock Matt off his chair and have him scrambling across the floor like a bug. Harry smirked to himself as he pictured it. Harry, however, was not his brother. He was the peacekeeper. The gentle one. Not an alpha.

"I'm sure we can work this out. Perhaps I can delay the tour a couple of days. I'll need to make a few calls."

"I don't care what you have to do. If Sabrina isn't able to do the tour, I'm not going." Matt rose to his feet and stared at Harry with a dark look as if daring him to argue. The two of them had been talking for two hours, eating into Harry's day. He glanced at his watch and gave Matt a nod in defeat.

"I'll update you in the morning. Just try not to worry."

Matt strode across the room like he owned the place, swaggering his hips and moving his arms dramatically. A petite woman entered the room, blushing at Matt as he passed by.

"Mr. Jackson, you are expected at the Tower in twenty minutes," she said in her strong New Yorker accent.

Harry rose to his feet and checked his watch again.

"I still have time," he muttered to himself. "Thanks, Amy. Please get my publicist on the phone."

"Yes, sir."

Harry clasped his hands together and shrugged in his tailor-made suit jacket. He hated wearing a suit. In fact, he was known to turn up on the red carpet in a pair of denim jeans and a relaxed chambray shirt. As a producer, he got away with the style, but attending an event at Lincoln Center had strict requirements. The cheapest seats were over $400, and with the sizeable ticket price, a formal dress code came with it.

His meeting ran over as usual, forcing Harry to send Benjamin to collect Julie from her apartment. He stood outside the entrance to the opera, a dozen cameras flashing repeatedly, blinding his vision. A babble of chatter filled the air, but he didn't care. He was so used to the attention, it was as if they were not even there. Minutes rolled by as Harry waited patiently, looking up at the starry night sky. He counted the twinkling lights one by one, seeking out the constellations he recognized. His eyes were tracing out the Big Dipper when a familiar rumble of an engine pulled him out of his thoughts. The flashing lights were no longer facing him but on the black Rolls Royce that had come to a halt outside Lincoln Center. Harry's face lit up as his heart rate accelerated. His driver Thomas, a tall slender man with very little hair atop his head, gracefully got out of the vehicle and walked to the back door. Excitement and intrigue buzzed through the paparazzi as they anticipated who it might be. Thomas looked over and offered an expectant smile; Harry nodded to him to carry on.

Harry's breath caught in his chest and his heart thumped against his rib cage. One long bare leg appeared, then another, as the pair of gold-glittered stiletto shoes sparkled in the street lights. Her long cream gown flowed down as she exited the car and the shoes disappeared from view. Thomas' narrow frame partially obscured Harry's view as he watched a slender hand grasp the sleeve of Thomas' black jacket.

"Who is she? Who is it?" one of the reporters asked loudly to the others. The clicks of the cameras buzzed along with the multiple questions from the paparazzi. As if one giant spotlight beamed down on the woman, Thomas moved aside, and Harry wanted to fall to his knees.

She is breathtaking.

The cream-colored dress hugged every curve of her body. A slit to the side revealed the lower half of her right leg, and the V-neckline showed just enough flesh to make any man sweat.

But Harry was not looking at her body anymore, he was transfixed under her gaze—sure that she could give him any command and he would willingly obey. He was utterly charmed. Her eyes were two glowing amber flames. Intense, and inviting. The curve of her lips rippling upward until her cheeks were plump like strawberries he wanted to savor. The image sent tingles down Harry's spine. He gulped so loudly, he was sure it could be heard even over the noise of the paparazzi. With an air of entitlement, they barked questions at Julie. She didn't owe them anything. Harry stepped forward automatically and offered his arm to her.

"Hello," she said softly, sliding her hand through the crook of Harry's elbow and squeezed his bicep. He flexed under her touch, his muscles tightening instinctively. Her hair was swept up into a loose bun with wispy flyaway hairs framing her porcelain face. Long thick lashes fluttered as her eyes darted around the intrusive paparazzi.

Harry thanked Thomas and sent him on his way; he bowed in response and returned to the car. Benjamin must have exited the car and was now standing still, holding open the doors and nodded to Harry as he and Julie walked past.

"Joseph and Martin are already inside. The box is

ready for you," he said in a low voice, now they were out of earshot of the press.

Harry nodded in acknowledgement and rested his hand on Julie's; the warmth of her skin against his made him weak. He wanted to caress her face with his hands and grasp the back of her neck. Wild fantasies crossed his mind momentarily until Harry mentally shook himself.

Get a grip.

Harry guided Julie into their private box, and they settled down in the plush velvet cushioned chairs. They had a perfect view of the stage and the sea of people in the audience below. Harry turned to Julie and watched her stare at the theatre with her mouth hanging open.

"Have you been to the opera before?"

Julie looked at him, as if surprised by his question.

"No, never," she replied. Then after a thoughtful moment she corrected herself. "Once, but I was only a child. I hardly remember it."

Harry sensed there might be a story there. But before he could probe any further, the lights dimmed and the orchestra erupted into song.

Harry couldn't keep his eyes off her, as she stared at Catherine Fisher, a world-renowned opera singer, who entered the stage to a round of applause. Catherine was a star and the reason why the show had been sold out for months.

The music was enchanting. The melody rose and fell following a whimsical, beautiful story, floating up to the tall ceiling, lifting the energy. Harry's head was fuzzy, not only with the music but seeing her hand resting on the arm of the chair, so close to Harry's wrist. His fingers twitched as he wrestled with the urge to take her hand in his. He leaned in to whisper in her ear, the flowery scent of her perfume drove him crazy.

"Are you enjoying it?"

Julie turned her head, a little too quickly and her nose bumped against his cheek. She blushed and automatically raised her hand to Harry's cheek. He wanted to close his eyes and savor the moment.

"Sorry," she blurted and removed her hand. Harry swallowed against a dryness in his mouth. Catching her off guard, he took her hand and rubbed his thumb across her smooth knuckles. Bolts of electricity shot through his arms and straight to his heart. The chemistry between them was like nothing he had ever experienced before. Julie's eyes widened as she looked at him, the two of them hovering within inches of each other. Harry didn't blink. He didn't want to miss a moment looking at Julie. She stared back, as if daring him to make a move.

Harry did not plan to make out with Julie—especially in the middle of the opera! She was a lady. He was a gentleman. He had morals and respect. But she was so tempting and right within his reach, just a breath away.

He was not sure if it was the romantic, heart-soaring music that melted his resolve, or dim lighting casting an ethereal glow around her. But something made Harry forget his surroundings, and he was pretty sure they could have been in the middle of a tropical storm and he wouldn't have noticed. All he knew was that Julie had her eyes locked on him and nothing else mattered.

"Do you mind if I—?" Harry didn't finish. There was no need. Julie leaned forward and claimed his lips in the sweetest kiss he had ever known. Her lip gloss tasted like cherry; it was addictive and her lips were softer than rose petals.

Harry pressed his forehead against Julie's and the two of them sat like that with their eyes closed, absorbing every gorgeous moment. The symphony of music and Catherine Fisher's melodic singing sent them away to their own magical world.

Harry was known to fall in love quickly. He promised himself that after last time, he would keep himself on guard—have fun, but be careful with his heart.

And yet here he was. With Julie's delicate hand against his chest and her lips pressing against his temple. When she drew away and blinked slowly at him, her cheeks were rosy. Harry decided there was no hope left for him. She had his heart. Every part.

Before his rational mind could stop him. He found himself willfully obeying the impulsive, passionate side of his mind. Without any hesitation, not even a tiny moment of consideration, Harry slid out of his chair onto his knees and looked up at Julie with imploring eyes. He grabbed her hands in his and pressed them to his lips before looking up again.

"Marry me."

Julie's eyes grew wide. She blinked at him a few times in a stunned silence. Then, her entire face grew red. Suppressing the urge to jump to her feet and scream with joy, Julie said the first thing that came to mind.

"Sure. Why not?"

CHAPTER 9

Madly in Love

Julie decided that the opera should come with a warning sticker.

Careful, heart-stirring music may lead to impromptu proposals.

In the moment, it seemed entirely ordinary to be proposed to. The fancy clothes. The gorgeous music. The mood lighting. It was all a perfect setting to pour out your heart in song and declare your true love.

Yet, Harry quite literally fell to Julie's feet and said the last two words she thought he'd ever say. To her, at least.

"Marry me."

And in her shock, she came out with the only thing that sprang to mind, which just so happened to sound like she accepted his proposal.

Rationale did not return at the end of the show. Nor did logic rear its head when Harry and Julie sat in the back of the limousine driving around New York. In fact, the romantic urges only intensified. Now they had some privacy, the heat ramped up and hands started to roam. They were two souls beautifully entwined as they followed wherever their passions took them. The limousine came to a stop outside Julie's apartment and Harry and Julie broke apart panting and sweaty. Julie's heart fluttered faster than the wings of a butterfly and she became dizzy, grinning at Harry, as if the pair of them had behaved like a pair of mischievous youths.

Harry hesitated. He looked like he was going to grab her behind the neck and pull her in for another kiss. But his hand froze in midair, and he shook his head with a casual smile.

"Are we crazy?" he asked.

Yes, completely crazy. But I don't care, thought Julie as she surveyed his face. His hair was disheveled and there were blotches over his forehead.

"Maybe," she said quietly.

"You know, I don't even care," Harry said with fervor, taking her hands in his. "I've never felt this good."

Julie couldn't argue. Sure, this was their second date and three days ago the two of them were complete strangers, but Harry's hands were familiar. His kisses were grounding and equally thrilling. The tone of his deep voice and the warmth of his skin against hers made her feel like she had come home. She had never experienced anything like it before. It were as if she was Helen of Troy and he was Paris in a previous life, and they had found each other again.

"I feel like I know you," Harry said, he gripped her hands tightly and stared at Julie with a total look of vulnerability. This was not just a pick-up line; she was sure of it. Julie's heart soared.

"I know exactly what you mean," she whispered, tracing a line down his neck to his collarbone. The touch seemed to lower Harry's defenses once more and he lunged forward. Julie leaned back against the leather seat as Harry rested the palms of his hands on either side of her. His shoulders rounded and his face lingered millimeters away from hers. He was like a hungry lion and she was his prey. Willingly, she closed the gap and the tension between them reached new dizzying heights.

A vibration broke the two apart. Harry looked down at his leg. As he sat back, Julie took the opportunity to recover herself. Her skin was on fire, as if someone just dialed her sensitivity levels up to maximum.

"Remember, I asked you to come with me to this charity event?" Harry asked, looking up from his phone.

"Yes," Julie nodded as she gingerly touched her throbbing lips. Harry eyed her.

"Did I mention it's in London?"

No. He didn't mention that.

Julie suppressed the urge to gasp and planted a fixed smile on her face.

"England? Great, I'll be able to see my parents."

"I wondered if you were British. The accent," he said, leaning forward and smoothing Julie's hair with tenderness.

"I'm sounding more American every day. But I thought you'd pick it up, seeing as you are too."

Harry shook his head. "I'm not British," he said firmly.

"But you said you went to—" Julie began. Harry raised a hand in the air, as if about to offer up his darkest secrets and Julie fell silent again.

"I said I went to boarding school in England. I didn't say I was born there."

"Oh that's right, sorry. Where did you say you were from again?" Julie asked, blushing profusely. She had been so preoccupied with gazing at Harry's perfectly chiseled face that she hadn't paid much attention to their dinner conversation.

"My parents were born in Canada, then settled in Idaho. After their divorce, my mother married an English diplomat and they live in Surrey now."

"So, you're kind of British?"

Harry's face reddened as he laughed.

"How does that make me *kind of British?*"

Julie chuckled back.

"I don't know," she said simply. "But you're not really Canadian, are you? Not if you were born in Idaho and grew up in a British boarding school."

"I suppose." Harry rubbed his chin and looked down in thought. Their heated moment had passed, and Julie looked awkwardly out of the window. An endless stream of raindrops poured against the glass, and she inwardly groaned at the thought of running up the steps to her apartment.

My dress will be like a pile of old rags by the time I get inside.

"Can I walk you to the door?" Harry asked gentlemanly. Julie snapped her head back to him and raised her brows.

"In that?" she gestured to the window with her thumb. "I hardly think there's any reason for us *both* to end up like drowned rats."

"You're right." Harry looked thoughtful again.

"We'd have to get out of our wet clothes before we catch a cold."

Julie opened and closed her mouth like a fish out of water.

"Mr. Jackson! I have standards, you know."

Harry grinned sheepishly. "Sorry," he added quickly. He bent down and pulled out a black umbrella from under his seat. "Now, if you would allow me to walk you to the door, I promise that neither of us will be like drowned rats."

Harry stuck to his word. He expertly shielded them with the black umbrella in the rain as Julie picked up the skirt of her gown and tiptoed up the stone steps. At the door stop, she turned to face Harry, pressed up against his chest, and craned her neck to look at his face.

"Thank you," she said a little louder than usual. The rain hit the umbrella like a beating drum. It was not as fast as her heartbeat, though. "So, when will I see you again?"

Harry's eyes creased as his mouth curved upward. He took his free hand and caressed Julie's cheek.

"Not soon enough," he replied.

Smooth.

"When are we going to England? I'm not the boss, like you are. I'll have to ask for time off." Julie offered a playful grin as she walked her fingers up his sleeve.

Harry rested his hand over hers and his eyes moved side to side as he looked into Julie's eyes with adoration. They were like two long-term lovers sharing a tender farewell.

"The event is Saturday night, we can leave late Friday and be back before Monday."

That'll be the shortest visit I've ever done.

"Right," she said brightly. Harry took her left hand and rubbed his thumb across her bare ring finger before lifting it and pressing it with his lips. The skin burned where he touched her, as if she had been branded.

"I'll send across some details later and see you soon." His silky voice was enough to make any woman swoon. His face looked like it had been expertly carved out of rock. Chiseled, angular, irresistibly handsome, with deep-set eyes and a strong brow. Julie traced her fingers around his brows and down to his cheekbones.

"Do you…." Julie hesitated. She was going to invite him in, but she wasn't sure she wanted to. Not only did her cat not like men and would hiss and launch a claw attack without hesitation, but she had emptied the entire contents of her wardrobe into her living room. She didn't want to bring Harry in to see that.

Harry made the decision easy. He pecked her on the cheek and pulled her in for a warm hug.

"I have to go," he said softly, though he took her

keys from her fumbling hands. He tried each one until the door finally clicked.

"Thanks again, it's been a... magical evening," Julie said with a sigh. She opened the front door and they both turned when a strange noise alerted her to stop moving. A hissing sound followed by the rush of stomping feet.

"What on Earth...?" Julie bent around Harry's torso seeing the limousine sitting innocently in the rain. The loud hissing faded and the driver got out of the car. One of Harry's security guards had dashed up the steps to join him, his face flushed and alarmed.

"I'm sorry, sir, it was just a kid. None of us had reason to suspect...." He trailed off before brandishing a piece of paper to Harry, who stood like stone holding the paper firmly in one hand.

"Did someone slash the tires of your limo?" Julie gasped. As if nature intended to add dramatic effect, a flash of lightning lit up the dark sky and a low rumble followed shortly after. Harry's eyes were like two tiny slits as he studied the paper in his hand. "What is it, Harry? What's that writing?"

Harry swallowed and looked at Julie as if he had seen a ghost; he then turned the paper so she could read the words scribbled with messy handwriting.

You think you can have her? Over my dead body.

CHAPTER 10

Suspicious Intentions

"**I**s that a threat?" Julie's question and accompanying wide eyes told Harry everything he needed to know.

Julie knew nothing about the first note.

Whoever was sending these clearly had a problem with Harry dating Julie, and the person had not been threatening her specifically. How anyone was able to slash the tires with Benjamin's whole team within the vicinity was beyond his comprehension. He shot Benjamin a look before turning back to Julie, who stood frozen in the doorway.

"I'm very sorry to ask, but seeing as there is no sign of this rain letting up anytime soon... can I come in?"

Julie blinked at him like he was speaking a foreign language, and her face paled. He wasn't sure why his question was being met with stunned silence, especially after he'd already done a crazy off-the-cuff proposal and suggested a last-minute trip to England. But for whatever reason, allowing Harry inside to keep out of the rain seemed to stun her.

"Or, we could just stand in the lobby while I wait for the tire to be changed. If that makes you feel more comfortable."

Julie stepped inside and nodded, apparently lost in her own thoughts. Harry handed the umbrella to Benjamin. "See if you can help Thomas. The last thing we need is a driver with the flu."

Benjamin eyed Harry shrewdly as he took the umbrella, and after a moment, nodded in resignation. Harry knew that a lecture was forming. He no doubt would become subjected to it later.

"Harry, look at me." Julie's alarmed voice was like an iron fist squeezing his heart. This was the very reason why he didn't mention the first note. Harry looked at Julie; her face was resolute, but her amber eyes gave her fear away.

"Why do you not seem surprised by this?"

Harry bit his lip as he deliberated whether to tell

Julie the truth. It would only worry her more, but looking at her expectant face caused his heart to ache. She deserved to know. Besides, he was a terrible liar.

"This is not the first threat I've received," he said grimly.

Julie gawped at him. "What do you mean?" She looked him up and down, as if suspecting Harry might have more threatening letters on his person.

Harry tried to sound calm and grounded as he told Julie about the note he received after their first date. He tried to convince her that he had everything under control and there was no need to overreact, but Julie was having none of it. She drummed her fingernails against her hip as she paced the hall.

"How do you know they're talking about me?"

Harry resisted the urge to laugh.

"Well, I don't see any other ladies around me."

Julie folded her arms and stuck her hip out to the side. Her bottom lip protruded—sensually—and Harry momentarily forgot what they were talking about. Her hair was falling out of its bun, and he couldn't get the image of removing her hair clip and watching a cascade of curls fall down to her waist. The thought made his mouth dry.

"I'm just a seamstress. A nobody."

Julie's words struck a chord in Harry. His eyes smarted and he blinked in disbelief.

"How could you say that?" He took a step and grasped her hands. She was not a nobody.

"You know what I mean. I'm not rich and famous. I'm no threat to anyone." She tilted her head and blinked up at Harry with a look of seriousness. Harry softened his gaze and slid his hand through her hair to rest at the back of her head. The touch made Julie close her eyes as she leaned into his hand.

"Sir, the car is ready."

Harry jumped back and Julie's eyes shot open as if Benjamin's return had broken a spell.

"Right." Harry patted his legs and looked from Benjamin's disapproving face to Julie's look of worry. "Now, you're not going to freak out about this, are you?" he asked Julie, pointing to her.

"Only if you don't," she quipped back, folding her arms again. "Besides, now is your chance to—"

A loud ringtone interrupted their conversation. Harry apologized and took his phone out of his pocket.

"Sorry, hang on." He took the call. "Mother, everything all right?"

"I wanted to make certain you were coming to brunch on Saturday. I have Oliver making all the arrangements." Harry glanced at Julie, who was studying her fingernails, as if to give the impression she was not listening in on the conversation. Even though he had not put the phone on speaker, his mother's loud voice barked at his ear.

"Yes, I'll be there."

"Good, and are you still bringing… what is her name again?"

"Julie," Harry said quickly. Julie's eyes flickered up to meet his before she blinked away and studied the notice board on the wall.

"Ah, yes, Julie. Is she still your date?" Harry couldn't decipher his mother's tone. He eyed Julie as he weighed his options. They would need extra security, he figured, and Benjamin would need to investigate the letters and now the damage to his car. For all he knew, Julie was in danger, and until they found out more about this mystery threat, it would be best to keep her close by.

"Yes, Julie will be with me."

Harry's mother hummed like a purring cat before she spoke. "Marvelous. Well, Gordan and I are looking forward to seeing you and meeting your… Julie."

Harry ended the call and Julie looked up at him expectantly.

"Do you have any crazy ex-boyfriends I should know about?"

Julie dropped her hands from her hips and gave Harry a hard look. It were as if he had just uttered an insult. Benjamin cleared his throat.

"I need to go. I'll call you tomorrow?" Harry motioned to take Julie's hand, but she took a step back and bit her lip, her face wracked with worry. Just minutes ago, they were making out in the back of the car like a pair of teenagers, and not an hour before that, he asked her to marry him. Now she was flinching away from his touch. Harry set his jaw and gave her a nod instead, then he turned on the spot and followed Benjamin out into the rain, still hoping he had a fiancé.

H arry sat at his desk with his head in his hands. It was not the first time someone tried to sabotage his happiness. When he and Ebony were together, an influx of threatening text messages came rolling in. Her over-bearing big brother Martin never liked Harry.

"My little sister doesn't need to be with a wet blanket," he sneered, his bulbous nose dripping with perspiration, and the veins in his neck bulging after an intense boxing session. Ebony thought it would be cute to have her boyfriend and brother bond over working out at the gym. But it was more like a weekly torture session, where Martin took the opportunity to pick at Harry's character, tearing him to shreds. The look of sheer delight on his face was forever burned in Harry's memory when the news broke that Ebony had been seeing Phillipe on the side.

"Now he's a guy who can carry his own," he said with approval. Harry was not raised to be an alpha male. He loathed to see the jerks roam around college on the prowl, looking to treat unsuspecting ladies like dirt. Yet, somehow, the sensitive and genuine guys—like Harry—never ended up with the girl.

Even in the real world, long after graduating, Harry discovered it was still like the animal kingdom—a hierarchy among men. Who got the girl. Who landed the promotion. Who claimed the last parking space.

Being a billionaire producer only helped in the sense that Harry had been able to hire a whole team of professionals to keep him safe—and their "leaks" about Harry's tough character garnered him respect.

Yet, conceited actors often made ridiculous demands that he knew his fellow producers would not put up with. Christian Bones had been black-listed by every director and producer in the business, and Harry was the only person willing to take him on. Christian refused to show up to set if his mocha double latte was not piping hot or if his lucky cap had gone missing, but Harry knew a lot of actors were superstitious, so he postponed shooting for an entire week while they searched everywhere for Christian's Yankees cap. It turned out Christian wanted an excuse to visit a girlfriend in Maine. The cap mysteriously reappeared on his return.

Harry rubbed his temples and grimaced at the memory.

Why am I such a pushover?

It wasn't like he wasn't warned. His advisors and coworkers had told him to expect Christian to pull a stunt. But when it happened, he refused to see if for what it was. His biological father was the same way. He raised Harry to always assume people had good intentions. Be the nice guy. The sensitive, caring guy.

Harry pushed against the mahogany desk and sat back in his recliner chair.

And look where that got you, Dad. Your wife had an affair, took half your wealth, and ran off to England with another man.

The papers said Harry's father died of a broken heart. Harry wondered if that were true. Or maybe he had been too soft for this cruel and harsh world.

Someone was trying to threaten Harry into submission, only this time it wasn't a conceited actor, but someone willing to carry out a threat. He had no idea who this new adversary was, and his instincts told him to back away, leave Julie and find a nice, simple relationship. The note was troubling, but slashed tires took the threat to a new level. He considered how much the situation could escalate. Was she really worth the hassle?

The image of Julie standing in her gown, nipped in at the waist and hugging every curvature of her body, appeared in his mind's eye. Her delicate hands clasped together and bottom lip protruding, her pretty face framed with white-blonde curls hanging down her spine, her two big amber eyes glowing, the image warmed his heart and quieted his worries, and a sense of peace and calm stirred his soul. There was something about her that made Harry... different. She made him want to try and be a better, stronger person.

He rose to his feet in the empty office of his downtown apartment. The only light in the room came from the streetlamps outside.

"I'm going to take her to England," he said firmly, staring at the grandfather clock on the wall. "And, I'm going to marry her." He grinned to himself. A rising fire burning from within his chest. Just then, the door swung open and a flood of light filled the room, blinding Harry.

"Sir, permission to speak candidly." Benjamin stood in the doorway framed in the light. Harry's shoulders slumped as he made eye contact with him.

"All right, Benjamin, what is it?"

"I respectfully advise that you do not see Julie

Andrews again, at least until we have ascertained the culprit of these recent... events."

Harry heaved a big sigh and lowered to his chair once more. He tapped the desk lamp and it lit up the desk. A soft yellow glow illuminated the lower half of Benjamin's face. His mouth a perfect straight yet very tight line.

"I'm not scared of some silly notes and a kid pulling a stunt." Harry mustered his best casual smile, but Benjamin merely looked back, his face set.

"Do you have any idea who could be behind this?" his head of security asked. Harry rubbed his chin in thought.

"It's got to be someone linked to Julie, an ex-boyfriend perhaps? I'm hoping you can figure it out?"

To Harry, whoever was behind the threats was either clever or old school. Handwritten notes given by random people and a kid to slash the tires of the car—there was no paper trail to follow. If it had been text messages, it would have been easier to trace, or if the guy faced Harry himself.

"I'm guessing you are going ahead as planned, then." Harry detected a slight tone of defeat.

"I love her," he said fervently.

"Sir, forgive me... but you're *infatuated* with her. Love is quite different."

Harry shrugged. "I don't care what you call it. I'm not leaving her. We're *supposed* to be together."

The corner of Benjamin's mouth twitched. "Do you think it's wise to talk about marriage so soon? It has only been—"

Harry rose to his feet and clenched his fists.

"I know what you're thinking. I know how it looks. But I can't help the way I feel."

"I understand, sir," Benjamin said carefully. "I am merely considering Julie's feelings. You don't want to scare her off, do you?"

Harry faltered.

"Do you think she thinks I've come on too strong?"

Benjamin raised his hands and shrugged. "I'm just saying, people don't usually ask someone to marry them on their second date."

Heat rose to Harry's forehead. He rubbed the back of his neck and paced the room.

"I don't know what happened. It was like I wasn't in my body and I just—"

"Got carried away, sir?"

Harry stopped pacing and slumped his shoulders. He stood less than two feet away from Benjamin and looked at him square in the eye.

"All right. I'm listening. Tell me what to do."

CHAPTER 11

FOOLISH LOVERS

"Are you crazy?" Emily burst out with her hands on her hips. She stared at Julie like she just announced that she was moving to Mars.

It was the next morning, and Emily had brought over breakfast, clearly as an excuse to catch up on the gossip. Harry had declined the other dates Emily planned and settled the invoice. Now that he no longer wanted to be contacted through her agency, Julie was her only source of information. And the mystery was clearly killing her friend.

Julie wondered whether to let Emily know about

the events of the previous night. She gave a play-by-play on the photoshoot; how it went at the opera, how beautiful the orchestra played, the stirring songbird voices, and the heart-pounding tension between her and Harry.

She casually mentioned Harry's proposal when Emily exploded.

"Look, I know I set you two up, but Julie… you've only been on a couple of dates." She strutted around the room with her hands in the air.

Julie bit her lip. She hadn't even reached the truly worrying part of the story. How would Emily react when she learned that someone was actively threatening Harry, even vandalizing his car to keep him away from *her*.

Emily eyed her with scrutiny before she continued. "I'm all for romance. You know that. But it must have been a joke, right?"

"Why would he joke about it?"

"Why would he ask a stranger to marry him?" Emily shot back. Julie cast her eyes to the carpeted floor and chewed her lip. Emily didn't understand. Of course, she didn't.

That's just it… we're not strangers.

She considered telling Emily that they were old souls. Because that's exactly how it felt. A couple of old friends reunited after many years; although, there was nothing platonic about their friendship. Her cheeks warmed at the thought of Harry grasping her back when they fooled around in the back of the limo.

"Did something happen between you two? You're blushing."

Startled, Julie blinked up at Emily and tried to shrug it off. "I'm not blushing."

"Then why is your face red?"

"I'm sick," Julie said.

Sick of this conversation.

"So, how did you leave it? Are you going to this charity event? Did you find out where—"

"London," Julie cut in. Emily stopped pacing the room and stared at Julie with surprise.

Emily Stewart had perfect brows. Expertly shaped and extremely expressive. Julie often marveled at how they appeared to move independently of each other. Today, they danced through all sorts of positions as she internalized this news.

"Are you flying together? Probably in a private jet, no less." She flicked her hair back and arched her back as she looked up at the ceiling, as if expecting to see through the top of the building and spot Harry's private plane.

"So, he's taking you to England." She rested her chin on her hand as she paced the room again. Julie could almost see her mind racing with thoughts. "Well,

I can't say I'm surprised he's fond of you. I mean, I am the highest-paid matchmaker in New York for a reason." She smiled to herself. "But I don't like how serious this is getting. As your best friend, it's my duty to let you know when you're making foolish choices."

Julie sighed.

"I know." She studied her fingernails to buy herself time to think of a proper response. Emily was right. They were moving too fast. Or maybe they weren't, and the proposal *was* a joke. Maybe she'd made their relationship out to be far more serious than it really was. Her thoughts turned to the threats. Who they were coming from? Were she and Harry better off calling it a day and going their separate ways? She needed someone to talk to about it, someone to help her work out her options.

Resolved, Julie took a deep breath and looked up from her nails to Emily's expectant face. "That's not all... Emily, I need to tell you something."

J ulie slumped back in her chair and rolled her head from side to side as she rubbed the back of her neck. The steady hum of the sewing machines in the hall was so loud she wasn't sure if her ears were actually ringing.

The simple clock hanging up at the top of the hall looked sterile in the room. Eight minutes until she could go home—or until she finished the hem on the skirt she had been working on all day. There were about ninety workers sitting at their own machines, in rows silently getting on with their work. The tiny windows let in very little sunlight, which did not offer the best lighting for Julie's work. The department was tucked away in the basement; Estelle's dirty secret. This was not *Project Runway*.

Frank prowled up and down the tables, his narrow eyes flitted from desk to desk, looking for a reason to fire someone on the spot. He loved two things; drama and being in control. He was also quite fond of peppermint tea. The minty aroma followed him wherever he went, and he almost always complained of a stomach ache.

Julie figured that Frank loved to stir up drama so that everyone couldn't think about anyone other than him. Behind the harsh look on his face, Julie saw a pair of fearful eyes, probably dreading the day someone called him out for who he really was. A fraud.

Julie watched him approach a small woman with bright red hair. She was slumped over her desk immobile; she'd evidently caught his attention. He stopped one foot away from her desk and leaned toward her with rounded shoulders like a lion creeping up in its prey. The slow and steady rise and fall of the woman's back told Julie that she might have nodded off—an easy thing to do with the steady sound of machines whirling like white noise. Yet an unforgiveable offence in Frank's book.

Had Julie been any closer, she would have kicked the woman's ankle or something. But being two desks behind only offered her a perfect view of a situation that was entirely out of her control. The sounds of the machines dissipated as everyone—including Julie—understood what was about to go down.

"Ms. May," Frank snapped. The woman's ginger hair nearly stood on end as she jumped. "I'm sorry. Was I interrupting a *siesta*? Pleasant dreams?"

"I'm sorry, my daughter is teething, and I didn't get much sleep last night—"

"Oh, interesting. So, you think it is acceptable for Estelle to pay haggard mothers to catch up on their shut eye?"

Julie clamped her hands over the edge of her seat as her blood boiled. She imagined herself charging across the room to the woman's defense.

She remained frozen in her seat.

The woman was crying now. Her whole back wobbled as she mumbled her apologies. Frank straightened and curled his lip. His eyes glinted.

"Don't let it happen again," he said with a sneer. The room as a whole sighed with relief.

Crisis averted. There will not be any firing today.

Satisfied the danger had passed, Julie returned to her skirt and finished sewing the hem. She resisted the urge to look up as she sensed Frank walking, his peppermint fumes lingering. She looked up expecting to see him gone, but he was standing over her desk. A rising sense of nervousness caused her muscles to stiffen.

"A word with you in my office."

Julie glanced around the hall. Though Frank spoke in a low voice, she noticed the room's attention was now on her. A silence hung in the air like a dark cloud. Julie swallowed and rose to her feet and followed Frank, who was looking at the floor.

It was a long, slow walk to Frank's office. Wild scenarios flashed across Julie's mind as she attempted to work out what Frank wanted to speak to her about.

"You've won the company lottery. Here's a check for one million dollars. Noelle loved your work so much, and she wants to hire you as her personal seamstress."

She was not sure which scenario was less likely.

They reached the small office and Julie stood in the same spot she was in when Noelle burst into the room the day before. Frank took his place at the leather seat behind his desk and lowered himself down like a king. He gestured for Julie to take a seat opposite. She obliged and rested her hands in her lap, waiting for her fate.

"I want to make it irrevocably clear that you broke a serious company policy." Frank poured a drink and surveyed Julie over his glass. She eyed the tangerine-colored liquid, as he swirled it around, then swallowed.

"Are we still talking about the dress?" she asked. Frank put his glass down and closed his eyes for dramatic effect.

"The materials in this building belong to Estelle. Employees are not to take anything home. Not only could something happen to damage the product—"

"But nothing happened, it was fine. Noelle—"

"Don't say that name in here." Frank opened his eyes and glared at Julie as if she had uttered the worse curse word known to man. Julie fell silent and pressed her lips together to stop herself from humming with disapproval. Frank picked up his glass and stood. He turned his back on her and looked out the large window overlooking Central Park.

"Belligerent. That's what you are."

Julie's mouth fell open. Frank was known to be paranoid about his position, always thinking the workers were plotting mutiny. Julie could not fathom how he came to the conclusion she was hostile. Did she not do everything he asked? The dress was fine. Noelle got what she wanted. The photoshoot went ahead and she even helped with that too. And when he shouted at the poor mother moments before, she held her tongue and just watched.

"You have a total disrespect for rules and company policies. And you often have a look of contempt."

Flashbacks crossed Julie's mind as she remembered Emily telling her she could read Julie like a book.

"I always know when you're mad at me. You have a look of thunder on your face."

Julie chewed her lip and curled her fingers, digging her nails into the palms of her hands.

"I'm sorry, Frank, it won't happen again." She tried to sound genuine. But her skin was burning, it were as if her blood had come to a boil and was now evaporating through her pores.

How can he stand there and say these things?

"You're officially on probation. If you step a toe out of line, you're out that door. Do you understand?"

Julie nodded. Her head thumped as the sound of her heart beat drummed against her ears.

"Yes, Frank. I'm sorry."

Julie swallowed again. Trying hard to stop the rant bubbling in her chest. She wanted to tell him he was a jerk. No one liked him. He treated the staff so poorly, she had a mind to go to HR about it. Perhaps she could get ahold of Noelle, she would be quite happy to dispose of him.

"Now get out." He chugged the drink and slammed the glass on the desk.

Julie collected her things and left the building without speaking to anyone. She would often keep to herself in the office. The other staff gossiped in the kitchen or hovered around each other's machines when Frank went on his breaks, but Julie kept her head down and avoided making conversation. It wasn't that she didn't like people, she just didn't like being *around* people. Making friends, striking up chit chat, and maintaining conversation were exhausting activities. Emily understood that. She accepted Julie's awkwardness, perhaps even loved her for it. Usually Julie would pick up the phone and call Emily at times like these. When her emotions had risen to the surface, and she didn't know what to do about it. But this predicament would mean letting Emily know that her job was less than perfect, that her boss was a nightmare to work with, and that deep down she wanted to give him a piece of her mind, spill his peppermint tea over his desk, then leave for good.

But Emily wouldn't understand. Julie would be subjected to another rant—and she just suffered an extended one about staying away from Harry. When

Julie filled her in on the threats, Emily started to speak so rapidly that Julie could only catch a few words.

"Police… creepy… get the heck out!"

Julie shuddered. No. She didn't need another Emily rant, and her warnings against Harry only made him more enticing.

He was now the forbidden fruit.

And she was hungry.

As if the universe had answered her wish, Julie's phone vibrated in her bag. She pulled it out and glanced at the screen. A grin flashed across her face and she answered the call.

"I was just thinking about you."

CHAPTER 12

AGGRESSIVE NEGOTIATIONS

Harry rubbed his temples against the migraine starting to form. It had been a long day. The press tour for his upcoming movie was finally back on track. His team was able to rally and get Sabrina to rejoin the group. Harry didn't ask how many prescription drugs it took to get her to agree to it; he didn't want to know. With Sabrina back onboard, Matt was happy, and that was all that mattered.

The London premier was scheduled the day after the charity dinner. Harry wondered whether he should take Julie to such a public event. *Going to London will get us out of the country, so surely the mysterious threat won't follow us to England,* Harry thought.

Benjamin firmly advised that he leave Julie in the US and go to the charity dinner alone. It might be for her own good, but Harry couldn't bear the thought of seeing his mother and having to put up with her disappointment, nor would he turn around and tell Julie not to come. No, he couldn't do it. Harry was a man of his word.

He silently apologized to Benjamin and picked up his phone.

"I was just thinking about you."

Harry's heart warmed at the sound of Julie's gentle voice. "You were?" he asked, his voice a little too high to sound normal. "I was wondering if you were busy tonight." He tried to sound casual, but his elevated heart rate made him feel dizzy with excitement. Just the idea of seeing Julie again had him grinning ear to ear.

"I've had a murder of a day at work. Whatever it is, I'm in."

Harry walked Julie toward the glass doors of his exclusive gym with his hands covering her eyes. Julie chuckled and reached out blindly ahead of her as they stumbled forward.

"Is this really necessary?" she said through a laugh. Harry was beaming, her perfume flooded his senses, and the warmth of her body so close to his sent rushes of excitement through him. Harry knew the best remedy for a frustrating day at work—his brother had pounded that lesson into him for years, having owned his own gym in England. Benjamin rolled his eyes as he pulled open the glass door and watched Harry walk through with Julie in front of him.

"I hope I don't end up walking into a wall," Julie said with a hint of reproach in her voice. "Why does it smell like feet? Is that workout music?"

The steady beat of the music echoed in the gym hall. There was a mirrored wall to the far side and every work-out machine stood like trophies in the room. Harry removed his hands from Julie's eyes and keenly watched her, excited to see her reaction. She blinked a few times to adjust to the blinding lights that reflected off the shiny white flooring.

"Oh wow." She marched forward a few steps and stood resting her hands on her waist in a superhero pose. Harry's eyes lingered on the back of her head;

her white blonde hair was pulled back into a high ponytail revealing her elegant neck.

"When you said 'work through our frustrations,' I thought you meant go for a run around Central Park." She turned to face Harry and folded her arms.

"Are you kidding? Jogging in Central Park is dangerous for normal people—"

"Oh, that's right, you're not 'normal,' you're a millionaire," Julie teased. But automatically raised her hand to her mouth as soon as the words came out, and her wide eyes made Harry think she had spoken too soon.

Billionaire, technically. But who's counting?

Harry blushed furiously. "The carriage ride was risky, even with the security, but I don't think I can chance it with a run out in the open." Harry offered a casual smile as Julie stared at him. She stood rooted on the spot, looking cute in an oversized blue shirt and black leggings. Harry thought she looked stunning in formal wear, but seeing her in casual clothes made her look even more tempting. She stood there looking like at him with no idea just how badly he wanted to hold her up and kiss her.

He snapped out of his daydream and gestured to the large, black punching bag hanging in the center of the room.

"I come here when I need to release some tension.

You know, when you deal with people all day and don't get to say what's really on your mind."

Julie hummed and nodded in response.

"Shall we?" Harry asked politely as they walked to the punching bag. He stooped down and picked up a pair of boxing gloves and handed them to Julie. "Here, put these on."

Julie obliged, glancing at Harry with a look of amusement as she did so.

"All right. Now what?" She stood with her arms hanging limply at her sides; it looked like a pair of bowling balls replaced her delicate hands. Harry walked behind the bag and asked, "Okay, so tell me about Frank."

"He's a—" Julie's voice faltered, she bent to the side and her face came back into view. It was flushed as she considered how to finish her sentence.

"—moron?" Harry offered. Julie's face broke into a grin.

"Yes," she said firmly. Her head bobbed as though cementing the fact. Harry clapped his hands together and pointed to the bag.

"Okay, Frank is a moron. Now throw everything you've got into this bag."

The bag jostled side to side as she pummeled it, alternating fists and huffing. Harry raised his brows and clapped.

She's done this before.

"Tell me, what did you want to say to him today? When he was picking on that woman? What was her name again?"

"I don't know." Julie sounded breathless. "Isn't that terrible? I should know the names of the people I work with." She threw herself into another burst of punching. "I wanted to walk up to him and say, 'Frank, you're a jerk. Stop treating everyone like your servants. Nobody likes you. If you just tried to be more like a leader and less like a dictator—'" She threw more punches into the bag. Harry nodded along.

"Nice. I like it. Go on."

Harry walked around and watched Julie really get into it. She threw punches and smashed her knee into the bag for extra effect. Tirades of shouting and angry yelling followed. The sight took him by surprise, and he knew his brother would be seriously impressed.

"I had no idea you had so much anger inside of you," Harry remarked as she slumped with one arm around the bag and took deep breaths. Her face was blotchy and shiny with perspiration. Her blonde hair was frizzed at the hairline.

"Neither did I," Julie said while panting.

"You know, the other night… at the opera," Harry began as he rubbed his neck. Julie eyed him carefully and straightened her back.

"It's all right. I know you were just joking," she said with her hands raised.

"Joking about what?"

"Oh, you know, the whole 'will you marry me' thing? It's okay. I was just playing along."

Harry resisted the urge to clamp his teeth against his lip but set his jaw instead.

"Right. What a relief," he forced himself to say after a moment. Julie was studying his expression now; he tried to fashion a causal smirk.

"I mean… we just met," she added carefully.

Harry nodded along and broke into a false laugh, his heart sinking. Maybe Benjamin was right; it was only infatuation between the two of them. He needed to cool off and act casual if he had any chance of spending more time with Julie. He figured one more intense move would have her running for the hills.

"Right. I do want to spend more time with you though," Harry said. Already forgetting his own promise to play it cool. He braced for Julie to eye him warily. Her beaming smile set his worries at ease.

"It's a good thing too. We're going to England in two days." She pulled off the gloves and wiped the sweat off her forehead with the back of her hand. Seeing her looking so confident and pumped with adrenaline sent flutters of excitement in Harry's midriff.

"You know, Frank really is a moron. And if he gives you any more trouble, I want you to tell me. I know Estelle and—"

"Oh no," Julie said waving her hands and shaking her head at Harry. "You're not doing that."

"Doing what?"

"The 'I'm going to step in and save the day' thing. I don't need you to fight my battles for me."

Harry stared at Julie blankly.

"I know that," he said honestly. "You're the real deal, aren't you?"

The question sent a flush of color to Julie's face, and she tucked a strand of hair behind her ear.

"I just have to raise the courage to speak to *him* face-to-face… and not this punching bag."

CHAPTER 13

WHAT HAPPENS IN LONDON...

J ulie spun around in the salon chair to face the mirror and gasped.

"It's so short!" she said, running her fingers through her silky-smooth hair. The stylist furrowed her colorful brows. Clearly, this was not the reaction she was hoping for. Emily however, clapped and made sounds of approval.

"It's still touching your shoulders, you look gorgeous."

Julie leaned forward to inspect the roots. A beautiful platinum shade of blonde once more. No more evidence of her true mousey hair color showing through.

Harry was due to pick her up in a few hours. Emily insisted on taking her straight from work to Fifth Avenue for some last-minute shopping, and she booked Julie an appointment with her stylist. Emily *loved* a good makeover. Although she disapproved of Julie's decision to go to England, she put aside her judgment and focused on the task at hand. Mission: make Julie look like a celebrity.

They had their nails done, brows threaded, and Julie finally found out what a Hollywood wax was—which she was *never* getting again. She winced as she shifted in the chair, still sore.

"We've got just enough time to grab dinner. Where do you want to go? We look so fabulous; it'll be a waste to grab take out and hide in your apartment." Emily glanced at her phone and chewed her lip as she thought.

"And yet, that's exactly what I want to do," Julie said with a sigh. She thanked the stylist and collected her shopping bags while Emily handed her card to the lady at the cashier.

"If that's what you want, I suppose you'll be dealing with a lot of public appearances over the next few days."

Julie groaned.

"Don't remind me."

The thought of turning up to a charity dinner with all sorts of wealthy people made her feel sick. There was also the endless list of "what if" scenarios crossing her mind. Harry didn't let her know where she was staying, who they were going to meet, what to expect, nothing. He just said, "I'll take care of everything. Just bring yourself... and clothes."

Julie did not like the unknown. But she figured if everything went badly, she could give her parents a call and crash at their house.

I should drop by and see them anyway.

Emily spoke at top speed as they walked onto the subway and got a seat, surrounded by their bags. Julie daydreamed about Harry as Emily's words floated over her head. The wobble of the train rocked Julie into a sleepy stupor, and before she knew it Emily snapped her fingers in front of her eyes. Startled, she jumped back and blinked at her.

"It's our stop. Come on."

The two of them pushed their way through the crowd of people at the subway and climbed the steps, heads bowed low. Rule number one: avoid eye contact and do not draw attention to yourself.

Julie wished she was carrying bargain bags. She and Emily were walking targets. Her friend had insisted on checking out the designer stores, and Julie spent so much money she was worried her credit card would set on fire. If it did, it would be for her own good. Though, she was going to have to live off mac and cheese for the rest of the month until her next pay check.

"But that Betsy Johnson bag is so gorgeous," Emily reasoned as Julie stood in the store looking at herself in the mirror, a black and white polka dot satchel at her side. "It would be a crime not to get it. Besides, it's just over a hundred dollars. It's not like you're splashing out on Gucci is it?"

Julie sighed. Usually she would suggest a bargain hunt in Jersey in all the outlets. But there was something about buying a bag full price that sent thrills through her.

They climbed the steps to Julie's apartment, grumbling at the weight of their purchases, and burst through Julie's front door. Emily dropped her bags to the floor and collapsed on the two-seater couch. Tabby meowed angrily and darted from underneath a chair to the back of the room.

"Tabby is so weird, you know," Emily mused, kicking her shoes off and rubbing her feet. Julie shook her head with a smile and closed the door.

"I know right. Trust me to end up with a dud cat."

Tabby was a rescue. The little old lady at the center said that no one wanted him because he was so skittish.

He was going to be put down that afternoon, which broke Julie's heart. So she adopted him. She suspected that he was abused by a man, because any male who came to the door was met with violent hissing and back arching.

"Now, promise me you will keep me posted the whole time you're in England. If I get radio silence, I'm sending out a search party."

"Yes, I know." Julie rolled her eyes. Emily perched herself on the edge of the couch and eyed Julie seriously.

"I mean it. I've done background checks on Harold—"

"Harry," Julie corrected. Emily inclined her head.

"He seems okay, but we don't know who this weirdo is who is following you guys."

"Emily, Harry has a whole team of security. I couldn't be anywhere safer. Nothing is going to happen—"

"I still don't have a good feeling, you know, and I always trust my gut."

"Oh yeah? Like the time you were convinced a spider was crawling on your back?"

"There *was* a spider on my back. You didn't see it because it jumped away."

"Right, and spiders can totally jump."

Emily launched into a rant about jumping spiders

as Julie smiled at her, nodding every now and then to show she was listening.

But she wasn't really listening, she was counting down the minutes until Harry rang the bell. Her stomach did backflips and her heart started to race.

Is this really happening?

The buzzer shook Julie out of her thoughts as a rush of adrenaline coursed through her veins. Emily stopped talking and grinned as Julie sped across the room and clicked the intercom.

"It's Harry."

Julie glanced back at Emily, who held her hands together excitedly.

"Come on up," Julie said, then crossed the room to collect her luggage.

"Emily, I feel sick."

"It's okay. I packed some Cinnabons in your carry-on."

"How is that going to help?"

Emily pulled Julie in for a hug and squeezed.

"Just be safe. I wish I could come with you, but Julian is sick and I have to take all his clients."

They broke apart at the sound of a knock on the door and Tabby launched onto the couch with his ears standing up and his back fur on end. Julie took a deep breath and opened the door.

Harry came into view, wearing a black leather

jacket and dark denim jeans. His hair was styled to the side and he flashed Julie a smile that made her go weak at the knees.

"Hey, there," he said smoothly. Then his eyes moved from Julie and widened. "Emily Stewart?" Julie turned to see Emily looking sheepish as she offered a little wave.

"You got me."

"How do you… Why are you…?" Harry seemed unable to find words to finish his questions. Before Emily could answer, Tabby jumped down from the couch and flew past Julie's legs right toward Harry.

"Oh sorry, my cat hates—" Julie broke off as she watched Harry crouch to the floor and offer his hand to Tabby, who was purring and rubbing his back on Harry's legs.

"Hates what?" he asked, looking up at Julie with his brows lifted. Julie glanced back at Emily and the two of them shared a look of surprise.

"Well, I'm not worried anymore," Emily said triumphantly as she rose to her feet.

"Worried about what? Why are you here again? I'm confused." Harry got to his feet with Tabby cradled in his arms like a baby.

"Me too," Julie added through a laugh. Emily walked past and rested a hand on Harry's forearm; her head didn't even reach his shoulder.

"Someone has to look after Tabby. And yes... I should probably have mentioned that Julie is my best friend."

Harry eyed Emily shrewdly, his lips pressed together as he murmured something inaudible.

"Well, here you go." He handed Tabby to Emily, but the cat's claws clung onto his jacket and Julie had to pry them off.

"Ready to go?" he asked Julie. She took one more look at Emily before turning back to Harry and nodding.

Let the adventure begin.

CHAPTER 14

Love in the Air

Harry reclined in the soft leather armchair, drink in hand and watched Julie take in their surroundings.

"What is this for?" she asked, pointing to a silver platter with a neat pile of steaming facecloths.

"You know, to wash your face and neck. The air is considerably dry in here once we're airborne."

Julie nodded along looking dazed. Then she turned and pulled out a fold-down table over her lap.

"I can't believe this." She took her sandals off and wriggled her toes with her legs outstretched. Harry caught himself smiling as he watched.

A young woman entered the cabin, dressed in a perfectly pressed blue uniform. "Good evening Mr. Jackson, Ms. Andrews," she said in Queen's English. Harry glanced at Julie as she straightened in her seat and slipped her sandals back on.

"The chef would like me to take your orders," the woman continued. Julie looked at Harry like a kid on Christmas day.

"Chef? Harry, this is so cool," she said patting her legs with excitement.

Harry liked this side of Julie. Out in public, she was quiet and a little awkward, as if not sure how to fit in. The nervous glances and slight disgruntled look on her face told him she hated being around people as much as he did.

Harry tolerated it. Understood that crowds, paparazzi, and attention came with his work. But he wished he could walk around incognito, without the security entourage and yelling men and women with their giant cameras.

"What's on the menu?" Julie's question pulled Harry out of his thoughts.

"What do you fancy?" he asked her. Julie shrugged and twirled her hair with her fingers. Was there something different about it? Her white-blonde waves were straightened out, yet it looked shorter. Julie drummed her lips with her fingertips in thought.

"I'm easy. I could eat anything right now." She rubbed her stomach as it growled.

"I'll have a filet mignon with a creamy mushroom sauce," Harry said with a nod. The woman smiled in acknowledgement.

"And you, Miss?"

Julie chewed her lip as her eyes shot to Harry before she grinned sheepishly at the woman.

"Can I ask for a slice of pepperoni pizza?"

"That's a great call. Forget a slice, bring in the whole thing," Harry added.

The woman left the cabin, leaving them alone once more. Julie reverted back to her relaxed self, sandals off again and slouched into her chair.

"So," she began as she swiveled her chair to face Harry. He resisted the urge to laugh. This new laid-back version of Julie was endearing and fun. "Has this plane got a TV?" she asked looking around the sparse cabin. A small cream leather loveseat sat facing a mahogany cabinet.

Harry picked up a white control and clicked. A large flat screen TV rose out of the cabinet and Julie clapped.

"This is the life," she said.

By the time the plane landed, Harry's cheeks ached, along with his stomach. The two of them binge-watched Julie's favorite TV show, one about werewolves and vampires, and consumed far more calories than Harry's nutritionist would like. The two of them relaxed together on the loveseat by the TV, Julie's head resting on Harry's shoulder, and all was right in the world.

It amazed Harry how comfortable he was with Julie. She was a breath of fresh air, grounding and authentic. In the plane, no one had to keep up appearances or worry about behaving a certain way. It was just the two of them, chilling out in a multi-million-dollar private jet.

Julie's response to the lavish lifestyle was refreshing. She acknowledged it, but dealt with it all in a healthy, curious way. It was as if Harry was experiencing it all for the very first time. It excited him to think about the weekend he had planned. There was so much to see, so much to do. He hoped they would get some time to be alone.

"What's our plan?" Julie asked as they got into the car that was waiting for them at the airport. Harry put his arm around Julie as she sidled in next to him. They fit perfectly together like two pieces of a puzzle.

"We're going to my London apartment to get ready. We are having brunch with my parents in a couple of hours."

Julie sighed.

"We should have slept on the plane," she said,

exhaling deeply. Harry rubbed her arm and hummed in reply.

"Don't worry, after brunch, we can go back and grab a few hours before the dinner. We can talk about it later, but I don't want you to worry about it. Once we're inside, there won't be any cameras. You've got to remember that these people, even though they have money, they're just… normal people." Harry found himself on a tangent. "Well, okay, some people can be pretentious and annoying, but the people at our table are mostly family or people who I consider family. You've got nothing to be nervous about." Harry stopped talking at the sound of a snore. He tilted his head to catch a glimpse of Julie's lashes touching her cheeks. He leaned back and secured his arm around her shoulders, squeezing gently as he looked out of the window. The English countryside rolled by as Harry grinned to himself. Of all the expensive treasures in the world, the one in his arms was the most precious.

CHAPTER 15

Meet the Parents

Julie stretched out like a cat, arching her back and yawning loudly. She patted the impossibly soft bedding around her and blinked into the sunlight streaming in through the white curtains.

She had no recollection of going to bed. She wondered if the last week was a dream and now it was time to wake up and finish that dress for Noelle.

The sound of busy traffic outside had Julie sliding off the strange king-size bed and marching across the carpeted floor to take a look. Big red double-decker buses rolled past the window, along with black taxi cabs and cyclists. The endless stream of traffic and the smoggy air had Julie beaming ear to ear. She was home.

Well, sort of.

She spun around to take in the room. A large white wardrobe stood in the corner next to a recliner chair, and an antique writer's bureau sat beside the bed with a desk lamp. Her luggage sat neatly at the foot of the bed, along with her sandals and her jacket lay folded on top of the bag. She looked down and wriggled her toes in the carpet pile and tried to recall what happened.

They were in the car. It was so warm and comfortable in Harry's arms. The steady beat of his heart was like the ticking of a clock. His chest rumbled against her as he talked, and the car vibrations sent her off to sleep faster than you could say "good night."

Harry must have carried me up to bed.

The thought sent butterflies to her midriff.

A knock on the door alerted Julie back to the present and she automatically called out. The door swung open tentatively and Harry's face came into view. He had dark circles under his eyes and his hair was tousled.

"Oh good, you're awake," he said in a scratchy voice. "We need to leave in fifteen minutes."

Julie's stomach lurched.

"Where are we going again?"

"We're having brunch with my mother."

Right. What does one wear to brunch with the potential mother-in-law?

Julie flashed a smile and offered a thumbs up as Harry closed the door. She turned to her case. Times like these had her wishing she smuggled Emily along too. But it was the still only the crack of dawn in New York, and Emily would definitely be—

Julie's phone vibrated, interrupting her thoughts.

"Why haven't you called me yet? I've been worried sick."

Julie's shoulders relaxed as she sighed. Emily's voice—although bossy and irritable—was music to her ears.

"Sorry, I fell asleep."

"You're supposed to stay awake. You'll never cope with the jet lag if you sleep all day."

Julie threw the phone on her bed and unzipped her bag as Emily ranted through the speaker.

"Tell me about the flight. How was it?"

"I don't have time, Emily. I have to be ready in fifteen minutes for brunch with Harry's mother."

There was a moment of silence. Julie wondered if the phone had lost signal, but Emily's voice came barking out of the phone once more.

"Fifteen minutes?" she screeched. Julie winced

against the noise. "How are you supposed to—" There was a huffing sound and Emily coughed. "Right, put on the yellow dress, use the donut thing to make your hair into a nice bun. Forget the lashes, go for simple makeup. In fact, you look gorgeous, just wash your face and put a touch of mascara on. Maybe a little gloss."

Julie nodded along as she pulled out a yellow jersey dress and held it up at her shoulders. "Is it cold over there? Wait, it's March and you're in England. Of course, it's cold."

Julie glanced out the window again.

"The sun is shining."

"Wear the white cashmere cardigan. Unless you think it will rain…."

Ten minutes later, Julie—with Emily's help—was looking fresh-faced and presentable. She found a tall mirror on the inside of the wardrobe door and inspected her work. She had carefully swept up her hair into a high bun at the back of her head and smoothed any flyaway strands with her fingers. The knee-length dress came out in an A-line from her waist.

"Thanks, Emily. This is great."

"Send me a picture, I want to see."

Julie snapped a selfie in front of the mirror and sent it to Emily.

"Yes, perfect. Now, don't forget the rules: stay away from politics, religion, and money. Compliment the house, but please for heaven's sake keep it cool, Julie. Don't gush. And be agreeable but have something to challenge too. You don't want to come across as someone with no opinions."

Julie's head was spinning with all of the advice, and she was feeling nervous once more. She never considered how to navigate a conversation with these people. Wasn't Harry's mother married to a diplomat? These were not the type of people she was used to mingling with.

"You don't want to come across childish. Don't do your usual 'oh this is so cool!' speech."

Julie's cheeks burned. She had completely let herself go on the plane. She gushed. She swooned. She did all of the things Emily told her not to do.

The problem was, being with Harry made her feel like she could just be herself. Maybe that was a bad idea, she wondered.

"Thanks, Emily, I've got to go."

"Good luck. Love you, Jules. You've got this."

There was another knock of the door.

"How are you getting on?" The door swung open and Harry made eye contact with Julie, his hand flew to his chest and he widened his eyes at the sight of her. "Wow, you look…" He pulled out an inhaler from his leather jacket and took a deep breath. "Breathtaking," he finished. Julie laughed.

"You look pretty good, yourself," she quipped back, her eyes hungrily taking in the sight of him. He wore a relaxed white shirt under his black jacket and a pair of dark denim jeans. He had gelled his hair in place and must have splashed cold water on his face; his skin looked bright and dewy again.

Julie's heart fluttered. The realization dawning on her that she was going on another date with Harry. They hadn't really spoken about it, but it felt an awful lot like they were a couple. How did that happen?

Harry held out his elbow. "Ready to meet my mother?" he asked smoothly. Julie slid her arm through his and together, they walked out the room.

Mature trees shrouded the gravel path a mile off the main road. Julie's heart raced as she looked out the window in a vain attempt to see what was ahead. Harry took her hand and squeezed; she turned to look at him, while biting her lip.

"She's going to love you. Don't worry. Besides, we won't stay long."

Julie tried to remind herself, she was just his date. Not a potential daughter-in-law. There was no need to be nervous.

"Right," she said determined.

The car pulled up beside a large, stone water fountain in front of an elegant country estate. The cream-colored house had climbing ivy near the front porch and more windows than Julie could count. It was like she was walking into a Jane Austen novel. This kind of home would usually be open to the public for tours. Farther along the path was a parking area full of expensive-looking cars.

"What a beautiful home," she remarked as they climbed the stone steps to the front door. Harry rang the bell and a woman pulled the door open instantly.

"Harold, darling, it's lovely to see your face." The woman had tight auburn curls and a narrow pair of spectacles balancing precariously on the tip of her nose. She was short, possibly shorter than Emily. Her inky eyes flitted to Julie before looking back at her son. The two of them embraced and shared pleasantries as Julie stood waiting. She wondered what the expectations were in this situation. Would Harry introduce her and she… offer a hand? Kiss on the cheek? Social etiquette confused her at the best of times, but high-class British etiquette was a whole different kettle of fish.

"Mother, this is Julie Andrews." Harry held his hand to the small of Julie's back, prompting her to step forward. Harry's mother eyed Julie as she made a small noise of surprise—as if she had not seen Julie standing there at all. Julie offered a hand just as Harry's mother clasped hers together.

"Hello, Mrs. Jackson, it's a pleasure to meet you," Julie said in her best impression of a *Downton Abbey* character. Her shaking hand sat hovering midair before she carefully lowered it.

"My dear," Harry's mother said with a slight incline of her head. "I haven't been Mrs. Jackson for almost a decade now. Heather Bowood."

Duh, Julie. One minute in and you've already put your foot in it.

Mrs. Bowood glanced at Harry, giving an exaggerated smile that did not reach her eyes.

"My darling, you did not mention that? I say, how little you seem to know about each other."

Julie marveled at how Mrs. Bowood reached that conclusion from the small mishap. She sensed a long visit ahead. Harry was wrong, there was every reason to be nervous, and from the strange vibes she was getting from Mrs. Bowood, he was wrong that his mother would love her.

"Well, please come in and meet the others." She turned on her heel and walked into the hall. Julie eyed Harry nervously as he gave her hand a reassuring squeeze, then closed the door behind them.

The house had tall ceilings and an oak staircase in

the center. An open fireplace sat on the right and as they walked past it, Julie's eyes took in the sight of the largest tapestry she had ever seen hanging above it.

"We're in the orangery," Mrs. Bowood said cheerfully. They walked through a newly renovated kitchen and into a room made up of mostly glass. A collection of patterned furniture sat around a large coffee table positioned in front of the garden. *Or gardens*, Julie thought. As far as the eye could see was English countryside. There were two people seated already, one was an older gentleman wearing a light grey suit—similar shade to the few hairs he had above his ears. A young red-headed woman sat, looking serene and elegant, with her hand resting on the gentleman's arm. As they entered the room, the young woman was laughing and flicking her hair back. The two of them rose to their feet and greeted Harry, neither of them acknowledging Julie's existence.

"Harold, good to see you. How was your flight?" the gentleman said. Harry hugged the man and turned to the redhead with a look of polite surprise. The color in his face drained and a vein in his neck bulged.

"Ebony? I did not expect to see you here."

Mrs. Bowood gestured for Harry and Julie to take a seat beside the redheaded woman. As they settled, she was grinning ear to ear. It appeared an evil plan was coming together.

"Oh, how rude of me. Ebony, this is Julie Andrews, Harold's friend," Mrs. Bowood said delightedly. She turned to Julie, her narrow eyes glinting behind the small glasses. "Julie, this is Ebony Holmes. Harold's former fiancé."

Ebony held out her hand to Julie. She was acting like the Queen herself, bobbing her heading and grinning in a similar fashion to Mrs. Bowood.

"Any friend of Harold's is a friend of mine."

Harry turned his head back and forth as if seated at Wimbledon. It seemed he could not decide who to look at. Ebony, his ex-fiancé , or Julie, his… *friend.*

Well, this just got awkward.

CHAPTER 16

TRUE LOVE

"Where is Phillipe?" Harry asked. Ebony's green eyes traveled down his body slowly as she bit her lip. He knew what she was doing in her imagination, and he didn't like it. Ebony Holmes was the last person he expected to see at his mother's house. When she left Harry for Phillipe, there was a mutual understanding between his mother and former fiancé that they were not on speaking terms. Harry wondered when his mother had buried the hatchet and accepted the cheating woman back into her life—and why?

"Phillipe and I are getting a divorce. We've been

separated for a while now." Ebony took a napkin from her Louis Vuitton purse and dabbed the corner of her eye.

"Phillipe had been spending a lot of time in Spain," Harry's mother explained in a low tone. "He's found himself a mistress over there. It's been quite traumatizing for Ebony."

Harry resisted the urge to smile.

That's karma for you.

"I'm sorry to hear that," Harry lied. He glanced at Julie. She sat with her back perfectly straight and a look of thunder on her face. He wanted to laugh. Clearly, she had never mastered the skill of hiding her emotions. She looked at Ebony like she was an offensive odor.

"Harry never mentioned you," Julie said to Ebony.

"Funny, Harold never mentioned you either... before this week," Harry's mother shot back in a silky voice.

This brunch was a mistake. Harry eyed his mother as he hummed. He realized now that on the phone she'd been trying to set him up with Ebony all this time. She didn't actually expect him to bring a plus-one to the charity event. And yet, a week ago he *wasn't* planning on bringing a plus-one and only invited Julie because he couldn't bring himself to tell his mother the truth. *What a mess,* he thought.

"So, Julie, tell me about your family," Mr. Bowood said evenly as he crossed one leg over the other.

"My parents are lawyers," Julie said, mirroring his body language. "They run a firm in London."

"Oh, so you're not from New York?" Harry's mother piped up. Harry watched Julie handle the conversation. A tirade of questions followed like arrows flying in her direction.

Julie explained that she grew up in London, an only child. And attended boarding school, where she went on to study at Oxford University.

"What year? I attended Oxford," Harry asked without thinking. Heat rose to his face as he looked around the people in the room. It was a question usually asked on a first date. Did he just let the cat out of the bag that he and Julie barely knew each other?

"It was after you were there," Julie said, waving a hand aside casually.

"What did you study? What you do now?"

Julie told them that she studied fashion and spent some time in Paris working for Estelle's Fashion line.

"Impressive. So, you're a designer?" Mr. Bowood asked mildly. Julie didn't answer right away, she appeared to be considering her options.

"Sure," she said finally.

Harry's heart sank. She didn't need to lie about her work.

They enjoyed tea and scones while Mr. Bowood led the conversation to politics. They discussed various views on Brexit, and Harry's mother shared some elaborate conspiracy theories. Ebony hummed in agreement and nodded along, while Julie sat silent, a polite smile on her face.

His mother was just getting into her theories around Area 51 when Harry decided enough was enough.

"Well, sorry we can't stay. We need to get ready for this evening," Harry said as he got to his feet, and everyone followed suit.

"I'll see you later." Ebony leaned in and kissed Harry on the cheek. A waft of her familiar perfume covered his body like a cloak. The once-appealing scent was now a stench that made him slightly nauseous. Flashes of memories crossed his mind's eye —of Phillipe and Ebony walking hand in hand. Laughing.

Harry secured Julie's hand in his and they left the house without speaking. The car waited on the drive and Thomas opened the door for them.

"Well, that was… interesting," Julie said as they fastened their seatbelts. Harry looked at her as she tucked a section of hair behind her ear and blinked back at him. With the sun shining in through the windows, her amber eyes looked more golden today.

The light reflected off her glossy lips and before his brain could stop him, Harry acted on instinct.

He shrugged off his jacket and wrapped his arms around Julie's small frame, starling her. He hugged her so tightly, she made a squeal. He loosened his grip and planted light kisses on her hair, then moved to her cheek.

"Harry," Julie said in a surprised tone. He nuzzled his face in her neck and ran his hands up and down her back. He needed to feel close to her.

"I'm sorry," he said finally, breaking away. The car rolled away from the house and bumped along the gravel path back to the main road. Julie's face was flushed and she looked out of her window with a grin. "You're right, that visit was… interesting."

Julie looked back and the two of them shared a silent conversation with their eyes. At least, that's what Harry thought was happening.

"So, Ebony was your fiancé? What happened?" Julie asked, her voice was pitched much higher than normal. Harry knew she must have wanted to ask the whole time. Perhaps that was why she didn't join in the conversation… in case it slipped out. Harry would have liked that, to see Ebony's victim act torn to shreds when he said to the whole room that he broke off their engagement because she was a cheat.

"She… wasn't who I thought she was." It was

oddly difficult to tell Julie about Ebony. Besides, on reflection, he had realized that the two of them were wrong for each other. She was high-maintenance and outspoken. Always barking orders to Harry and making excuses to be out in public, so they'd be featured in some gossip column alongside a Kardashian. It was a loveless relationship, yet at the time Harry didn't see it. He was so desperate to be loved that he was blinded by the fact Ebony was just using him for her own ambitions.

"I'm sorry I didn't tell your parents the truth." Julie's words interrupted Harry's thoughts. He rubbed his thumb along her cheekbone and studied the guilty look on her face. A small worry line had formed between her brows.

"I felt so small. To say I'm just a seamstress when your mum assumed I was a fashion designer... it was too humiliating." She averted her eyes.

Julie was the polar opposite of Ebony. She was sweet, funny, and gentle. Even when she was dishonest, she ended up confessing the truth. Harry's heart swelled and he leaned in to give her the softest kiss.

"I understand why you did it," he said as he broke away. He took her hands and pressed his lips against her smooth knuckles. "Just promise you'll never lie to me."

Julie pressed a hand up to Harry's chest, the

warmth from her fingertips radiated through his whole body. As if she had special healing powers, the ache in his stomach and flashbacks of Ebony dissipated.

"All right." Julie walked her fingers to his shoulder and squeezed. "Seeing as we're being honest, I want you to know. I don't think your mum likes me."

Harry laughed.

"Well, I do." He kissed her again. "In fact, you have bewitched me. You are all I can think about. Being with you is all I want." He pulled up the sleeve of her cardigan and kissed her arm.

"Me too," Julie said in revered tones. Her words were almost drowned out by the rumble of the car engine.

"I'm glad we met and I'm happy you're here." Harry leaned in for a deeper kiss when the car pulled to an abrupt stop. Harry and Julie jolted forward, then lurched back again.

"Apologies, sir." Thomas had rolled down the glass divider and his dark eyes were looking at Harry from the rearview mirror.

"Is everything all right?" Harry asked.

"Yes, sir, the security team are just clearing the road. No need for alarm. Just stay in the car." The tone of Thomas' voice did not make Harry feel settled. He had known Thomas for too many years to not know when something was wrong. A few years back, Thomas had tried to insist that there was nothing to worry about, when they were sitting in a traffic jam downtown. His voice was a little strained, and Harry discovered that a bank robbery was taking place, which led to a car chase around the city.

Harry patted Julie's knee before he took off his seatbelt.

"Stay here. I'm going to check it out," he said to Julie, who—not sensing any reason to be alarmed—gave a nod.

Harry pushed open the door and climbed out of the car. The gravel crunched underneath his feet as he marched to the front. The sun was hidden behind a batch of clouds and the air was eerily still. Benjamin and four of his men were standing in a line, immobile, looking ahead. Whatever they were observing was obscured by their forms.

"What is it?" he shouted. Benjamin turned, his face grim.

As Harry approached, two of the security staff moved aside and then he saw it. A giant piece of blue tarp was fastened to a pair of oak trees on either side of the road. It hung like a banner, sporting large words written in red.

Last warning. Leave her... or the consequences will be deadly.

CHAPTER 17

Dangerous Escalation

J ulie decided she couldn't just sit in the car and wait. Long minutes had passed and curiosity got the better of her. She got out of the car and tiptoed to the front to see why they'd been stopped for so long. She wondered if a tree had fallen or a farmer was crossing with a herd of cows. Either of those scenarios would have been plausible—and far better than what she saw. A couple of men in dark suits were untying a piece of rope, attached to a blue tarp. To the side lay an animal. At such a distance, she could not guess what it was exactly. Then she saw the writing, in dripping red ink.

"Is that blood?" she asked aloud. Harry had his hand to his head and turned quickly on the spot. His face drained of color.

"No, it's not." He hurried over to Julie, rubbing the back of his neck.

"But that dead animal… did someone—"

"It's fake. Just someone playing a prank," Harry said quickly.

"Don't lie to me, Harry," Julie warned. "That doesn't look like a couple of kids pulling a prank. It's a death threat." Saying the words aloud made it sound worse than it had in her head. Julie swallowed against the uncomfortable tightness in her throat. Who would go to such lengths to send a message to Harry? She thought they left the weird stalker in New York. But this message was clear. Whoever they were, they knew where Harry would be. Surely this was beyond the scope of what the media would do? Or a jealous fan?

"It's been staged. The goat is a prop. They used fake blood for the lettering, sir," Benjamin said as he approached. The men removed the tarp from the trees and folded it.

"We're collecting the evidence and will take it to the authorities."

"Shouldn't we have called them out here? Now there will be multiple prints all over it," Harry asked. Benjamin shook his head.

"No. We need to get you both out of harm's way. I'll deal with this. My team will escort you home."

Harry gave a nod and took Julie's hand.

"Right," he said. "Come on."

They returned to the car and Julie's imagination ran wild. They had been in the Bowood's home for almost two hours. Someone set this up, perfectly primed for their return. But who? An old school nemesis? One who now resided in New York as well?

"Do you have any idea why this keeps happening?" she asked Harry as the car pulled forward once more.

"No," he said. "I thought it was someone in New York, but now I get the feeling there maybe more than one person."

"But why, Harry? Why would anyone have a problem with you dating me?"

Harry looked thoughtful as he scratched his chin.

"Well, not to sound big-headed or anything... but I was named one of the top sexiest men in Estelle's fashion magazine."

Julie looked at him incredulously and resisted the urge to laugh. She couldn't be sure if he was joking or not.

"What has that got to do with anything?"

Harry shrugged and shifted in his seat. A dimple formed in his cheek as he grinned.

Julie took the opportunity to outline his face with

her eyes. His face was perfectly sculpted, as if by an expert. And his slightly wavy hair made Julie want to drag her hands through it. Her eyes lowered to his lips; they were becoming familiar to her now. Plump and smooth. Yes, she could see why Estelle named him this year's top sexiest man.

"You know, I've heard stories from these actors. Matt had a crazy woman send him some pretty vile pictures, threatening to do terrible things if he didn't break up with his girlfriend."

Julie opened her mouth, but no sound came out. After a moment she found her voice.

"So, are you telling me this is normal for you? 'Oh look, a dead goat with fan mail written in blood.' Just another day in the office?"

Is this what I'm going to have to deal with?

Suddenly, the idea of being with Harry felt uncomfortable. She wondered what Emily might say when she found out that they received a death threat. She'd go crazy. Probably fly over there and drag her back to New York, forbidding Julie from seeing Harry again.

"Whoever it is, they know where my parents live. I'm not sure going back to my apartment is wise either," Harry said. Julie looked out the window, watching the traffic pass by. She half-expected to see reporters hanging out of car windows and photographers wrestling with oversized cameras to get a shot at Harry.

"You're right," she said, turning back to him. "We need to go somewhere less… obvious." She bit her lip as she looked around the limousine. "And we need to go incognito."

"What are you suggesting? I get a pair of glasses and a fake moustache?" Harry quipped back with a smirk. Julie shook her head, her heart racing as a surge of adrenaline bolted through her body.

"We need to ditch the security, rent a cheap car, and—"

She broke off and pulled her phone out of her purse.

"And what?" Harry asked, a mixture of confusion and admiration on his face. Julie looked back at him resolutely and placed a hand on his.

"Time to visit *my* parents."

"**J**ulie, this is a surprise—a great one though. You must be Harry? Good to meet you." Julie's father shook hands with Harry and ushered them into the small mid-terrace. Julie inhaled the familiar scent of her father's sandalwood aftershave as he pulled her in for a tight hug.

Mr. and Mrs. Andrews were the most unlikely people to fall in love. They were opposing lawyers in a particularly nasty divorce court. The process took almost five years and when the proceedings finally reached its bitter end, Mr. Andrews asked the question no one saw coming.

"Will you marry me?"

The story was a family favorite at every get-together. Julie was never quite sure if they loathed each other or loved each other. Most of the time they had polar opposite views and enjoyed debating them. Julie's mother called it "healthy conversation." But to young Julie, it sounded like a pair of siblings bickering.

"Is Mum home?" Julie asked, looking around. A heavy bookcase covered the entire wall filled with law books. As a little girl, she looked up at the bookcase as it towered over her, wondering how many lifetimes it would take to read all of the volumes. She looked back at her father, his dark hair was greying on the top now, but his eyebrows were still bushy and jet black. He had a few more worry lines on his forehead. His almond-shaped hazel eyes seemed to smile at her, filling Julie with warmth.

"Sorry, no. She's in Scotland for work. If we had known you would be in town, we would have made arrangements." Julie's dad walked them through to the breakfast room. Comfy armchairs stood in a semicircle facing the large bay window to the front of the house. A beam of sunlight reflected off the mirrored coffee table and a grandfather clock ticked loudly in the corner.

"That's my fault, Mr. Andrews," Harry began. Julie's dad held up a hand and Harry fell silent.

"Please, please. Call me Charlie." He held a hand to his heart and gave a frank smile as they took their seats.

"Thank you. Well, I didn't give Julie a lot of notice about this trip."

Harry and Julie's dad talked for a while as Julie settled back into her favorite armchair with her feet tucked under her and listened to the low rumble of Harry's voice mingled with the familiar gentle tones from her father. Before long, the antique chessboard was out, and the two men struck up a game. Julie watched Harry pull off his jacket and roll his sleeves up, as her dad set up the pieces and the two of them exchanged playful banter.

There were no signs of concern on Harry's face. It was like nothing untoward had happened earlier. Julie, however, couldn't help but glance out of the window at the constant stream of traffic. Who was behind the threat? Did they follow them to the car rental? Was there any point going incognito? Maybe telling

Benjamin and his team to back off was a foolish plan? Benjamin said as much.

The comforting tones of Harry and her dad talking with the rumble of the traffic outside sent Julie into a sleepy slumber. She tried to resist, but jetlag took over and she found herself lost in sickly sweet dreams.

CHAPTER 18

It's for Charity

"When we get out, there will be a lot of press. Just follow my lead. We'll be expected to stand for a few pictures and then move along for the next arrival."

Harry squeezed Julie's hand reassuringly. Underneath the bronzer, he could tell her cheeks had paled and the idea of walking out into a big crowd was terrifying.

"What do I say if people ask me who I am?"

"You're my date," Harry said quickly. His eyes flickered down to her lilac gown. It had a sheer overlay with embroidered lilies on the skirt. The bodice looked like it was sculpted to fit her form, sitting snug on her shoulders with a soft bow neckline.

"I feel a bit sick," Julie said. Harry looked deeply into her eyes. They were like topaz, sparkling back at him.

"You look amazing. And once we get inside things will be a lot more relaxed."

Thomas pulled open the door and Harry stepped out. Screams from the crowd of fans behind the railings flooded his ears. The dark sky illuminated in flashes like bolts of lightning, as the press snapped endless pictures. Harry smiled at the crowd and offered a wave before leaning down to help Julie step out of the limousine.

As Julie came to a stand, her dress shimmered and swished with her movements. Her platinum hair was dazzling, held up in a loose knot with soft wisps framing her face.

She shyly waved a hand to the crowd and Harry guided her to the group of photographers waiting for them.

"Mr. Jackson, tell us, are you planning any more space opera movies?"

"Mr. Jackson, who are you wearing tonight?"

"Mr. Jackson, who is your date?"

The questions came from multiple directions and Harry forced a smile as his eyes attempted to navigate the sea of faces and blink through the blinding lights.

He looked at Julie. She stood poised, with her hand resting gently on her left hip, one foot forward. She turned to the side and leaned her shoulders toward the photographers while offering a coy smile. Julie dealt with the attention beautifully. Harry underestimated her; he thought she was too shy and reserved to deal with fame and attention. Yet, she knew exactly how to hold herself, how to walk, and when to ignore questions.

A staff member instructed Harry and Julie into the building. They were directed to a grand hall with over one-hundred circular tables. To the front was a stand, set up with a live band playing music as everyone took their seats.

"Oh wow," Julie gushed as she took in the room, pointing to various celebrities and speaking at top speed. She fell silent as a server poured their glasses, giving Harry an opportunity to speak.

"It's quite simple really, music, a few speakers, dancing…."

"Food?" Julie asked, sounding hopeful. Harry smirked.

"Yes, lots of food."

"Interesting, because I thought these people starve themselves."

"Only for special occasions." A tall Latina woman with long black hair flashed Julie a grin as she settled in the chair beside her.

"Oh my goodness, I know who you are—" Julie began but she stopped talking, holding her hand against her mouth. A flush of color rose to her forehead, and the woman's dark eyes flew to Harry, then she held out her hand to him.

"Harry Jackson. This is an honor," she said in a silky voice. They shook hands while Julie remained frozen, her eyes wide and flitting between the two of them.

"Nice to meet you—"

"Valentina," she purred.

"Rose. Valentina Rose. Harry, how do you not know who she is?" Julie rediscovered her voice and wagged a finger at Harry with a reproachful look on her face. She turned back to Valentina.

"I've watched all of your movies. I loved the vampire one with Luke Edwards. You two had amazing chemistry."

Valentina pressed her pointed nails to her collarbone as she gave a look of fake surprise. Julie struck up a friendly conversation with her and the two of them bantered back and forth while Harry sat there smiling like a drunk man. Two familiar men arrived at the table, one of whom had Harry rushing to his feet.

"David Marks? I didn't know you would be here."

David Marks was an old friend from school. The two of them attended Eton and then roomed together at Oxford. He was an architect and heir to the Marks Hotel chain. Harry liked that David kept out of drama and didn't treat him like a loser. He did call him Harold, though. Much to Harry's dismay.

"Hey, Harold, it's great to see you. Did you not get the email with the seating plan?" He dragged a hand across his jaw, then gave a polite smile and nod to Julie.

"Oh, you remember my brother, Edward?" David said pleasantly. His older brother was taller than David with burly shoulders and darker hair. The two of them shook hands and sat down.

"Have you met Valentina?" Edward asked as he pressed his lips against her cheek. Harry glanced at the empty chair beside him.

"Do you know who else is joining us?" he asked. David's face reddened as Edward elbowed him in the ribs.

"It was supposed to be David's plus one. But turns out he didn't have the guts to ask anyone out," he teased.

"Oh, that's too sweet," Valentina chimed in,

clasping her hands together as she fluttered her lashes at Edward.

The band stopped playing music and a gentleman stood at the microphone. The conversations in the room died down as the guests waited for him to speak.

"Welcome to the annual Sponsor a Child dinner." His voice boomed around the hall. Everyone clapped.

"First of all, thank you all for your generous contributions. Together, we have raised almost two million pounds to our charity." Further applause. "Please enjoy the food and the music. Later, we will open up the dance floor and there is a room set up with press for you to give your statements. Please remember to mention the charity, Sponsor a Child, and tell the press why this charity is important to you."

The man went on to give some statistics of all the children who had received support and aid thanks to the charity.

The Sponsor a Child foundation focused solely on supporting children who were born with disabilities. Caretakers, on call nurses, and support workers supported families who needed respite from the full-time care they provided. They also donated equipment and funds for a family holiday for low-income families. Anyone who was anyone booked a seat at this dinner— most likely because it was good for public image. However, David and Harry's motives were different.

"I can't help but think about Johnny," David said, holding a glass, his eyes glistening as he looked at the band.

"Who's Johnny?" Julie asked. Harry sighed as he turned to her.

"Johnny Princeton. He was a friend of ours at school," he explained.

"Was?" Valentina asked.

"Johnny was born with a rare genetic disease. His parents gave him the best education they could. He didn't board like the rest of us; there were too many hospital appointments."

"What happened?" Julie asked, her voice hushed.

Edward and David shared a look before Harry continued.

"He graduated from secondary school. We all went together to the prom." He smiled at the memory of Johnny in a wheelchair. "By that point, he was unable to speak, but his smile lit up the whole room."

Edward took over and explained that Johnny had died just before they started university. He was lucky to have parents with money, but the costs of care and giving him a quality of life had crippled the family's finances. They set up the foundation Sponsor a Child, and have dedicated their lives to sharing Johnny's story and helping families in need.

"That is so inspiring," Julie said when Edward

finished. She looked at Harry, tears in her eyes and squeezed his hand. "I had no idea."

"Why did I not know that?" Valentina asked, troubled. David scratched his chin as Edward rubbed the back of his neck.

"We don't talk about it, usually," he said frankly.

"But on the media, you come across as a player," Julie said. Edward chuckled.

"Harold? A player? David did you hear that?" He raised a napkin to his mouth as he laughed. David shook his head, laughing as well.

"Don't believe anything you read in the tabloids. They sell stories, not truth," David said wisely. "Harold is no more a player than I am," he added. Julie blushed and Harry knew she had her eyes on him the remainder of the evening.

The group of them enjoyed catching up, Julie and Valentina mostly talked to each other. Julie had her phone out and was scrolling through pictures for Valentina to look at.

"You are so talented. I adore this one. You designed all of these?" she asked as she flicked her sleek hair back from her shoulder. "I would love you to make me a dress for the Oscars."

Julie's hand flew to her chest as she gasped.

"I would love to," she said, breathlessly. The two women sealed the decision with a matching smile, when Harry took the opportunity to step in. He got to his feet and offered his hand.

"May I have this dance?" he asked. Julie's eyes flew around the room. Other people were taking to the dance floor, now that the food had been consumed and drinks were flowing. Julie hesitantly took Harry's hand and he pulled her up to a stand.

Harry rested his hand on the small of her back. Rubbing his thumb across the organza material and holding back the grin from taking over his face. All was right in the world. Among all of the supermodels and actresses, he was with the most beautiful woman in the room. Julie was a natural when it came to mingling with people. She had a comfortable presence about her, making people feel at ease. Yet, there was also an endearing shyness that made her even more irresistible to him.

Harry took Julie's hand and secured his grip on her lower back as they swayed in a circle to the music. Julie's soft hair draped across her head like a veil. A diamante clasp sparkled in the spotlights. The people around them faded away, and for a blissful time it was just the two of them in each other's arms. Comfortable. Close. Whole. He dipped his head to meet hers and when the song changed, they barely moved, their foreheads pressed together.

"I'm glad you came," he said softly. He wanted to

take her head into his hands and kiss her with every fiber of his being. Being with Julie was so right. So natural.

"Me too," Julie said quietly. She lifted her head and eyed him with a half-squint. "You're full of surprises, you know."

"Hmm. That makes me mysterious. I like that."

Julie gave an appreciative laugh.

Harry thought this was a good time to say something clever. To show off his outstanding intellect. His mind rooted through all his trivia knowledge, but before he could wow Julie with useless information, a tall man with the broadest shoulders he had ever seen tapped him on the arm. His eyes were as dark as ink.

"Mind if I steal your lady?" he asked in a tone that did not sound like he was expecting a response.

Yes, I do mind.

Harry swallowed as the huge man looked at him with an almost fierce expression.

"Of course," he heard himself say, though he was sure he didn't utter the words. It was as if he was working on auto-pilot and he couldn't help but be agreeable. The man grinned so widely his veneers shone like a flashlight in Harry's eyes. Blinded, he blinked and looked apologetically at Julie who had a polite smile on her face as he let go of her hand and moved away. The huge man held Julie a little too close for Harry's liking; he scrutinized Julie's expression for any sign of distress, primed and ready to step in. Then, a fake cough drew his attention, and a mass of red curls flooded his vision as a woman flung her arms around his middle.

"Harold, darling, I need to speak with you. This cannot wait any longer."

CHAPTER 19

Surprising Revelations

J ulie watched Harry leave the dance floor with
Ebony. The redhead wore a black fishtail dress
that made her hair look even more fiery.

"You may recognize me from *Bad Men*."

Julie turned back to look at the huge man who
smelled strongly of ginger. His face had so much hair,
she struggled to read his expression.

"Do you mean *Bad Boys*?" she asked. They sidestepped to the music, his hand was coarse and so large
she thought he could break hers if he squeezed.

"No, no. *Bad Man* is a spin-off from the movies."

Julie wasn't sure what else to ask as her eyes

scanned the room for Harry. Why did he go off with Ebony?

The song changed and everyone began dancing like they were at a nightclub. Julie took the opportunity to break contact with the man—she didn't even pick up his name over the sound of the music—and offered a weak smile before making her way to the edge of the hall.

Julie decided that Harry was not the type of guy who would go running back to his ex-fiancé at the first chance. She had nothing to worry about.

Yet, the two of them had only been dating for a week, and when a beautiful redheaded ex returned to Singleville, Julie couldn't *help* but worry.

Relax, Julie. He's just gone with her to... talk.

She thought she was crazy about Harry, but seeing him with another woman further cemented her feelings for him.

The tabloids had made Harry out to be someone he wasn't. Always photographed with ladies, scandalous stories about breaking hearts and getting into fights at the Oscars. Of course, none of it was true. Harry was the sweetest, most sensitive man she had ever known. Not that she had the opportunity to know many other men. The only male in her life outside of work was Tabby, and until now, she liked it that way.

As jealousy swirled around like snakes in her stomach, Julie wondered if *she* was being possessive and that perhaps she was overreacting. *Maybe it is completely normal to have your billionaire date walk away with his ex.* Then again—nausea rose to the base of her throat as she thought about it—maybe, she was perfectly within her rights to be annoyed. She walked out of the hall and followed the signs for the bathroom, her head spinning with scenarios. She reached the bathroom and pushed open the heavy door as she tried to stop the mental image of Harry and Ebony making out.

As Julie entered, one of the cubicle doors opened and Julie stood rooted on the spot, stunned at the woman who appeared in view.

"Hello, again."

The black sleek gown had diamonds sewn into the seamline, creating a beautiful outline of the woman's curves. Her thick red curls hung to her waist like a gorgeous mane. The woman stood a foot taller than Julie, making her feel like a child stumbling into a place she wasn't supposed to be in.

"Julie, right?" she added. Her unnaturally white teeth gleamed as she ran a tongue across them. Her eyes glinting, like Tabby when eyeing up a new toy to play with.

"Yes," Julie said, finally finding her voice. She moved to the sink and washed her hands. The scent of expensive perfume wafted over her as Ebony leaned into her shoulder and spoke softly into her ear.

"He's *such* a good kisser, isn't he?"

Julie's body stiffened and she clamped her jaw shut as she forced a smile.

"Do you mind if I ask a question?" she asked, fluttering her oversized lashes at her. Julie shook her hands and grabbed a paper towel, then turned to look at Ebony.

"You already have, but go on."

Ebony sashayed her hips as she waltzed around the bathroom, playing with her hair as she went on.

"How can you afford a fifty-thousand-pound plate?" Her eyes narrowed as she came to a stop and surveyed Julie closely. "You didn't really let him pay, did you? And please tell me what Harold is doing with a seamstress?"

Julie's heart quickened and sweat started to form on her upper lip. She tried to remain expressionless, but she always had a terrible poker face.

"Oh, yes. I know *exactly* what you are," Ebony sneered. "You think anyone bought that story about Paris? As if Estelle would notice you. Come on, admit it. You don't belong here."

Julie ground her teeth as her temper rose to the surface. She wanted to launch an attack and rip that beautiful dress to shreds. Some poor person would have spent hours, maybe even days hand stitching those diamonds, and Ebony didn't deserve it.

"I think that's none of your business," she said simply. Trying to sound like a school teacher reprimanding a child. Instead, she sounded like a whiny teenager trying to fend off a bully.

"It *is* my business. Harold and I have history, remember? We live in the same world." Ebony held her head high and started to walk around again. "You've known him for five minutes and think you've got him wrapped around your finger." She stopped and eyed Julie sharply, as if daring her to argue. When Julie remained silent, her satisfied smile returned, and she continued, "We both know Harold doesn't have a backbone. He'd never hurt a soul... to his own detriment."

"You're making him out like he's a pushover," Julie said bluntly, crossing her arms. Ebony's perfectly shaped brows raised.

"Well? And you don't think so? You're even more naïve than I thought." She looked away from Julie and studied her reflection with a sigh. "Most billionaires get to the top by earning it. Standing up for what they believe in and kicking down any obstacle in their way."

Julie's jaw throbbed as she set her teeth together. "Harold just got lucky. He ended up in the right crowd, had friends to back him on his little movie idea, and it boomed. Then the right person invested the profits in some high-risk, but high-return stocks." She pointed to herself and blinked to allow this information to sink in. She leaned in to Julie so closely her breath tickled her face.

"He would have *nothing* without me. He belongs to me—"

Julie inadvertently gasped as realization dawned on her. This confrontation was not Ebony fighting for the love of her life, she was looking for a claim on him. As if he were a Gucci bag she had cast away, then changed her mind.

"Wow. You're a piece of work," Julie said as she shoved past Ebony toward the door. "I'm done listening to this."

Ebony placed a hand on her shoulder.

"When it comes down to it, he won't *fight* for you, Julie. He just doesn't have it in him." She sighed heavily to add dramatic effect. Julie gave her the filthiest look she could muster.

"Comes down to what?"

Ebony inclined her head and blinked for a few moments, then offered strange lopsided smile.

"You really have no idea?" she said with surprise. "I didn't think you were *that* simpleminded."

She stepped aside allowing Julie to open the door.

Julie eyed the woman shrewdly, wondering what she meant, then left the bathroom, her blood boiling.

CHAPTER 20

Escape Plan

Harry strode across the hall smiling at people as he passed by, occasionally shaking hands with old friends, and nodding to people in the sea of faces. His mind, however, was spinning and his heart panged from his fruitless attempts to find Julie.

He didn't know why he followed Ebony off the dance floor. She had always been able to get Harry to follow her commands—as if she had him under a spell. While they were together he had found it endearing. Now, it was irritating.

Ebony would always present an ultimatum or dramatic reason for him to drop everything and run after her. Then, as if having a change of heart, she changed tact. Ebony said she needed to talk to him, and by the way she acted, he'd thought it was serious. Perhaps a death in the family or she needed help with money. But instead, she just took him to the edge of the room and stroked his arm as she looked out at the people on the dance floor. When she moved closer and rested her head on his chest he backed away.

"Ebony, nothing is ever going to happen between us again. I'm with Julie now," he said with his hands raised, hoping she got the "back off" sign. Ebony glanced around the people standing by them and looked tearful as she bit her lip. Then, without another word, she dashed to the ladies' bathroom.

Having given up looking for Julie, he wandered aimlessly along the perimeter of the hall, hoping that somehow she would find him.

And she did.

Harry stopped in his tracks as a beautiful blonde crashed into him. Her hands found his arms as she collided with his abs and Harry automatically lifted her up to stop her from face-planting the ground. Julie's face was flushed as she looked up at him, and Harry allowed a broad smile to invade his frown.

"There you are," he said, his heart exploding

with joy.

"Sorry," Julie said with a puff. "These heels...."

Harry smirked. The memory of their first date flashing past his minds' eye. A warmth flooded his veins and he found himself calming down. He stooped down and pressed his cheek to hers as he spoke into her ear.

"Do you want to get out of here?"

"You don't have to ask me twice. Let me just say good-bye to Valentina."

Harry and Julie returned to their table and found David sitting alone.

"Are you not up for dancing?" Harry asked him as he clapped a hand on his shoulder. David smiled politely before rubbing his thigh.

"I didn't bring a date. I imagine the men in this room would not appreciate me stealing their woman."

"A woman cannot be stolen, David." Harry wagged a finger at him. Julie stepped forward and offered David her hands.

"We were about to leave, but do you want to have a quick dance?" she asked brightly. David waved a hand aside with a sheepish grin.

"I appreciate the gesture, but you two go ahead. They're setting up the pressroom. You know, if you sneak out the back you might just miss all of that."

Harry clasped hands with David and they patted each other's backs as they said their goodbyes.

"Will you tell Edward and Valentina we say good-bye?" he asked. David nodded.

"It was really nice to meet you," he said to Julie as they shook hands. "You two make a perfect couple."

Harry took Julie's hand and squeezed. His heart swelling with pride. It was the first time anyone had called them a couple.

He liked the sound of that.

The two of them snuck out of the room like a pair of thieves. Tiptoeing along the hall and Harry opened a door for Julie to walk through.

"Excuse me, you aren't allowed back here," a burly security guard appeared in the doorway, startling them both. Harry pulled out a handful of pound notes. "I know, Henry, so if you let us out the back you'd be doing us a massive favor," he said. The guard looked surprised for a moment, then his eyes flickered down to his own name badge before he cleared his throat and took the money. Then he sidestepped out of their path and Harry tugged on Julie's hand.

"Come on," he muttered as they hurried down the darkened corridor.

"I can't believe people actually do that in real life," Julie said with a laugh. "Do you know where you're going?"

"Sure I do; this is the staff entrance," he pushed the emergency door open and the two of them crept out into the dark night. They were in a secluded parking lot with no press, no flashing cameras, no screaming fans. Just a couple of servers chatting by the dumpsters and a few parked cars.

"Now what? If we walk around looking like this, it'll draw attention." Julie pulled out the clasp in her hair and shook her head. A cascade of blonde waves fell to her shoulders and Harry stared—his mouth suddenly dry— transfixed. After a moment, he was struck with an idea and pulled his jacket off. Excited, he jogged up to the servers.

"Hi there," he said in a friendly manner. The female looked at him with wide eyes and her lips formed a thin line as if she was trying not to squeal. Though Harry couldn't be sure whether it was out of fear or excitement. He turned to the short male who had a mop of blond hair almost entirely covering his eyes.

"Do you think I could swap my jacket with yours?" Harry asked, he glanced at Julie as she caught up with him and looked baffled by the question.

"This is my uniform, sir. I'll be in trouble if I go back in without it."

Harry pulled out a handful of cash and stuffed it in his hand. The brunette gasped and jumped back as the male held the money in his hands like it was going to explode.

"This is more than I make in a week," he said in a reverent tone. He shakily pocketed the money and removed his jacket.

"Then I suggest you tell your boss you got sick and take this lovely lady out on a date." Harry grinned as they exchanged jackets. The brunette bent over laughing. The man shook the hair out of his eyes revealing a look of horror on his face.

"She's my sister, sir," he said. Movement in Harry's peripheral vision had him turn to see Julie with her hands covering her mouth and shoulders shaking.

"Oh, right," Harry said awkwardly. He thought he was doing so well playing Mr. Smooth. Then the facade came crashing down as he looked from Julie to the brother and sister and swallowed.

"Well, thanks. Is there anything else I can do for you, sir?"

Harry smiled and shook his head. Julie waved them off as the servers returned to the building. Once the door swung shut behind them, her smile disappeared, and she placed a hand on Harry's arm. Her eyes glowed a deep shade of yellow, as if reflecting the streetlights.

"Now we're alone, I have something to tell you,"

Julie said turning serious. Her brows furrowed as she looked at him. Harry tried to remain casual, but the urgency in her voice had him feeling nervous.

"Harry, I think I know who is orchestrating the threats and why."

CHAPTER 21

A Bump in the Night

Harry didn't believe Julie. She could see it in his eyes. She reprimanded herself for blurting out this sensitive information. Maybe she could have worded it better?

"It's Ebony. Your ex-fiancé is the perpetrator."

Yes, she realized she sounded like a character from a detective show. Julie was surprised she even came up with the word "perpetrator" at all. Words were not her forte, fabric was. But the pressing need to divulge this new discovery had been brewing from the moment she left the bathroom. The way Harry's eyes turned guarded, and his rolled his lips inward, then his jaw clamped shut had her convinced he thought she was making it all up.

As if I would lie about this.

"What makes you think that?" he finally asked, sounding far too diplomatic and calm. In her imagination, she saw him march back into the event, his strong arms swinging back and forth, and the veins in his neck bulging as he scanned the room for Ebony intent on bringing justice to all.

It was a nice fantasy….

Julie recounted the conversation she had with Ebony in the bathroom. Harry turned thoughtful, rubbing his chin as Julie paced and threw her hands in the air.

"And then," she stopped pacing and pointed at him dramatically, "she said 'one last warning, back off or I will destroy you.' Do you remember the way the first note was worded?"

Harry's brows twitched and his nostrils flared; he did the last thing Julie thought he would do under such circumstances.—he fist-pumped the air and kissed Julie so hard she almost lost her balance. His big hands were on her back again, pulling her toward him, creating a sense of security. It was as if his hands belonged there. For a few blissful moments, she forgot about Ebony, the threats, and even the fact they were standing in a deserted parking lot in the middle of London. If a savvy paparazzi thought to sneak around the back, they would have gotten some juicy pictures for the front cover of any magazine. In that moment, Julie didn't care. Harry's lips touched every inch of her face and neck, as his hands pulled her to his body. Julie was on fire. Her arms tingled, every touch magnified by the heat. Her heart pounded so fast she could hear it beating in her eardrums. She moaned. He moaned back. They circled on the spot, as if dancing again, as hands roamed and their passion took them to another realm.

When they broke apart, they were gasping like fish out of water. Julie's chest burned from the lack of oxygen. Who knew kissing could be so beautiful, and also so deadly? She never understood the term "kill them with a kiss." Now she did. All Harry would have to do was keep his lips planted on hers, moaning into it, and she would have been like a lamb at the slaughter.

It would be a beautiful way to die.

Julie pressed her fingers to her throbbing lips and grinned as her breathing returned to normal.

"What was that for?" she asked. Harry took her hand, pressed his lips to her knuckles, and held it to his heart.

"I've wanted to kiss you all day." He wrapped the server's jacket around her shoulders and planted a chaste kiss on her forehead. "Come on, let's go for a walk. We can discuss this mess later. Okay?"

Julie nodded, figuring he needed time to process this information. It wasn't every day you found out the person you were to spend eternity with wanted to destroy you.

Julie and Harry walked through the streets like a couple who escaped their prom early. People who came across them, barely gave them a glance; they were ordinary. Invisible, even. And that was exactly how Julie liked to be.

"This was a good idea," she said, squeezing Harry's hand as they reached the Thames. The moonlight flooded the surface of the water, it looked mystical. "I never thought we would be able to do this."

They came to a stop and Julie held onto the iron railing as they looked out at the boats on the water. A cold breeze flowed through her hair and she pulled the jacket tighter around her body. She leaned toward Harry and rested her head on his bicep.

"I'm not afraid of Ebony," Harry blurted out firmly. Julie lifted her head to study his face. He looked out at the water with his brows knitted together. "I'll admit, I was slightly worried earlier. Now that I know who it is… well, it's laughable, really."

He looked down at Julie and cupped her face. "You don't need to worry about anything." He said it so fervently, Julie almost believed him. It was great that he wasn't concerned, but knowing Ebony wanted his money and was willing to go to any extreme to get it filled her with doubt. She wondered just how far Ebony would go.

"Do you think we made a mistake coming here without your security?" she asked, glancing around them. The roads were busy with taxis, ferrying party-goers around the city. And the streets were noisy with men and women who had too much to drink. She looked back at Harry who was looking up at the moon.

"People go out without security all the time. Besides… it's not as if anyone will recognize me." He put his arm around Julie's shoulders and gently tugged at her hair. "For the first time since we met, I feel like I can relax." He smiled broadly at her. Julie found herself beaming back at him. She stared into his beautiful blue eyes, seeing the image of the moon reflected in them and leaned in for a kiss. The air grew still and quiet. Julie was lost in their moment, like in the movies, when everything fades away and only the lovers remain. As if they were the only two people in the world. But there was a little voice in the back of Julie's mind that told her something was not quite right. There was a lull in the traffic. She pulled back from the kiss. The street appeared to be empty.

A sudden movement caught Julie's eye, but before

she saw what it was, Harry cried out with surprise. He slumped forward and moaned then another loud thud had Julie jumping back and screaming. Harry stumbled as three dark figures wearing ski masks surrounded him —then the pounding started. Julie stood with her hands to her mouth, frozen in horror as they repeatedly hit Harry's torso.

Do something, Julie! Don't just stand there!

Her brain screamed at her to move. But she couldn't. Instead, she was forced to watch as the attackers took turns throwing their punches at Harry. Julie's ears rang so loudly she wondered if a steam train was nearby. Her senses came back to her on a sudden whoosh, and she took in a breath and let out the loudest, unearthly screech she could muster. The attackers stopped and covered their ears in response, giving Julie time to act. She lifted her dress and threw her right foot with as much force as possible to collide with one of the attackers' thighs, while ramming her elbow into the ribs of another. All of her kickboxing and boxing training came flooding to the surface as she moved. It did not matter that there were three of them. She was full of adrenaline now, and her fear was long gone. These people just attacked the love of her life.

They will pay.

She thrust her fist into whatever body she could reach; one of them fled the scene.

"Come on," another said in a muffled voice. Julie raised her elbows, preparing to defend herself, but the two remaining attackers limped across the road and disappeared into an alley. Panting and looking brazenly out at the street, primed and ready for another round, Julie waited. A couple of cars passed by. The eerie stillness disappeared and a scatter of people entered the street.

Julie's arms remained above her head, but she was trembling now. The danger had passed, and now a rush of emotions and adrenaline with nowhere to go came flooding back.

She silently thanked her parents for forcing her to attend self-defense classes the summer before she started university. It just saved her life.

A moan on the floor alerted her out of her thoughts. Julie crouched down to Harry and held his hand gingerly. His face was swelling up and blotches of red covered his hands.

"Are you all right?"

"Hurts to breathe," Harry whispered back, grimacing. Julie pulled her phone out from her bag and with trembling fingers, fumbled to call emergency services.

"Slow and gentle. Hold on, help is on its way," she said calmly, repeating the advice she heard on a medical drama she binge-watched over the summer. She remained controlled as she gave instructions for the ambulance and swallowed against the lump in her throat as she ended the call. Harry's breaths were quick and ragged as he lay on the ground, his head resting on Julie's legs. Her eyes prickled as tears threatened to fall, but she bit her tongue and blinked up at the sky as they waited for help to arrive. It was in that moment, as she held Harry in her lap and watched his chest rise and fall rapidly, that she knew they would never be safe. Ebony would stop at nothing. If she was willing to stoop this low, there was no telling what would happen next. Harry passed out and his breathing slowed. Julie cradled his head in her hands and looked up to the sky. Finally, she allowed tears to stream down her cheeks as she thought about what she had to do—for Harry's sake.

Resolved, she repeated the same mantra in her mind as she waited for the sirens to reach them.

Please don't die. Please don't die. Please don't die.

CHAPTER 22

LOVE AND SACRIFICES

Harry blinked into a bright light and wondered for a moment if he had died and gone to Heaven. The white light flooded his vision until he slowly recognized the figure of an angel standing beside him. It appeared as if the light came *from* her.

"Harry, can you hear me? Nurse, I think he's waking up."

The sound of her gentle voice was grounding and Harry found himself falling back into a sleepy slumber.

"Harold, darling, can you hear me?"

Harry inhaled deeply, a dull ache spread across his chest and he slowly opened his eyes. A machine beeped next to him and a hand squeezed his.

"Where's Julie? Is she all right?"

His eyes found the familiar sight of his mother sitting beside him. She pursed her lips and she stroked his face.

"She's just fine, darling. You were very lucky last night. If Ebony hadn't found you, I dread to think...."

"Ebony?" Harry burst out of his covers and sat up, then stopped to gasp for air. "She is not to be trusted." He rubbed his chest, remembering the beating he took. Looking over the line from his arm, he had enough strength to tug on the IV connected to the saline bag hanging beside his bed.

"What are you doing?" his mother asked, watching Harry pull the IV out of his arm and ungracefully swing his legs out of the bed. An alarm beeped and two nurses dashed into the room.

"Are you feeling okay, Mr. Jackson?" one of them asked. She had blonde hair, similar to Julie's, but her eyes were blue instead of the golden brown he'd come to love.

"I need to see Julie and speak to Benjamin." Harry pushed himself awkwardly to his feet and staggered to the armchair in the corner of the private room. His stomach throbbed and his chest screamed in pain as he grabbed the pile of neatly folded clothes and started to dress.

"Harold. She's gone," his mother said with a note of finality. Harry looked up and stared at her while the two nurses watched, as if considering what they should do. Harry's mother waved to them with a nod and gestured to the door, prompting them to leave. Harry fastened the buttons on his shirt, then with the grace of a newly born calf, stepped into his pants and stood up. He studied the look of concern on his mother's face.

"What do you mean, Ebony found me? Where is Julie?" He tried to keep his voice low, but the rising anger inside him was proving difficult to keep under control. His mother perched on the edge of the hospital bed and rested her hands in her lap.

"Ebony found you and Julie. You were unconscious with multiple injuries—though the doctor says they are minor and you were very lucky. Tell me, what were you doing walking the streets of London at night without security?" The sound of reproach in her voice matched the glare in her eyes. Harry ignored her.

"Where is Julie?" he repeated through gritted teeth. His mother shifted and glanced out of the window.

"On a plane, most likely," she said simply. Harry pushed his feet into his shoes, thankful they were slide-ons.

Of course, she's run away. I did nothing to protect her.

His heart raced and humiliation rose like heat to the surface of his cheeks as he clamped his teeth together and ground them with frustration. It happened too fast. One minute they were enjoying their romantic escape, looking up at the moon, and the next, he was pounded into the ground by a bunch of thugs. He couldn't even feel the punches that followed the initial one. Shocked and unable to process what was happening, Harry just took the abuse, but he remembered Julie. She'd turned into a real-life action figure and showed those attackers not to mess with them. If he wasn't so mortified at his inadequacy, he would have been prouder of her.

Now, she's gone. And she'll be too afraid to see me again.

Then again, Harry thought, maybe she wasn't afraid, maybe she decided that being with Harry meant dealing with too much drama. After all, with all the press and scandals that came with it—not to mention a psychopath ex—who would want to love Billionaire Harry Jackson?

He slammed a fist on his thigh and glanced out the window. The sun was shining like a summer's day, and the hustle and bustle outside reminded

Harry that despite everything, the world was still moving on.

"Harold…." His mother walked up to him and placed a hand on his back. "I hate to see you like this. Why don't you get back into bed and we'll sort this all out?"

Harry hesitated. He didn't know what to do. Should he get on a plane and follow Julie back to New York, profess his love, and insist they should be together?

But what if Ebony engineered more attacks? Even if he went everywhere with security, they would be forever looking over their shoulders.

Harry lowered himself back onto the bed and sighed. He needed to let Julie go.

"You know Ebony did this," he said dully to his mother. "Why are you talking to her again, anyway? After what she did to me?"

Harry's mother sat next to him on the bed and patted his knee.

"She loves you Harold. She made a mistake and wants you back. Can't you see that? You both have so much history—and she comes from a good family. Let's be sensible here. You two are good together, despite your youthful pasts."

"And you think we should pick things up where we left off? Pretend she didn't run off with Phillipe and then put a bounty on my head?"

"Don't be silly, Harold. No one's trying to kill you. I don't believe for one moment Ebony had anything to do with this. She is the one who found you."

Harry sighed. His mother would need hard evidence. Even then, she had a habit of putting her head in the sand and avoiding the truth when it hurt or it wasn't something she wanted to hear. Of course, she would be defensive of Ebony running off with Phillipe. Had *she* not done the same thing to Harry's father?

"You should never have brought Julie, you know. All of this would have been so different if you just walked away when you got that first—"

"Note? Is that what you were going to say? How do you know about the note?" Harry shook his head, shocked at this new revelation. "You had something to do with this?"

Harry's mother straightened her back and picked a loose thread from his collar. "I don't know what you're talking about. That is not what I was going to say." She refused to make eye contact.

"Benjamin said he thought a private detective was following us on our first date." He stood up and walked back to the window. "What I can't work out is, was he hired by Ebony... or by you?" He turned to face his mother, who looked back at him affronted.

"Harold Anthony Jackson, I did no such thing."

"Why are you so set on Ebony and I getting back together?" Harry asked, exasperated. Jonas had often accused their mother of being vindictive but pairing him with a woman who organized an attack on her son was surely a step too far. Even for her.

"Harold darling, I wish I could shake you by the shoulders and knock some sense into you. Ebony misses you. I miss you. We both want you to come home."

"So pick up the phone and tell me. Childish notes and messages written in fake blood are not the way to go about this."

Harry's mother looked at the floor and bit her lip for a moment. Harry wondered if this was a sign of regret or buying time to spin a story. She looked up at him and sighed heavily.

"I didn't know things between you and Julie were serious. Last week you didn't even know who she was."

"How did you know—" Harry stopped and scratched the back of his neck, struck by a thought. "You hired someone to follow me?"

"I worry about you. It's for your own safety. We both know you're a lot like your father—"

Harry balled his hands into fists and swallowed hard—as if being like his kind-hearted father was a bad thing.

"Ebony is strong, she has money, and she can keep you safe."

"That's ironic, because she's the one who just got me beaten up, and are you forgetting I don't need her money?"

Harry's mother sucked in air through her teeth in a hiss. "No one meant for you to be attacked. Why do you find it so hard to believe?"

"Well, someone did. And you've just confessed that the you two have been conspiring against me."

"Conspiring," Harry's mother repeated with a laugh. "It was childish. I will give you that. I only thought that if you sensed there would be confrontations and drama with Julie, that you would let her go and come home to—"

"You and Ebony are living in a fantasy world," Harry said frankly. "Single or not. There is no way I would ever get back together with her. Look what she's done. Just how far is she willing to go to stop me from being happy?"

Harry's mother rose to her feet and rested her plump hands on her hips, the way she did when he was a child and got into a fight with his brother.

"I've had quite enough of this. You need to rest. Ebony is coming to see you this evening. I expect you to be on your best behavior, and I will tolerate no more of this nonsense."

Harry couldn't decide if his mother's posh English accent was fake, or the result of living in England for years. Either way, it irritated him. And in that moment, he wanted to pick up a chair and throw it at the window. His own mother had been conspiring with his cheating ex-fiancé against him.

And Julie was gone.

It was fortunate that Harry's mother left without another word. His anger boiled so violently, he was worried what he might do if provoked even further.

Harry collapsed back onto the bed and pulled his phone out from his pocket. Nine messages, none of them from Julie.

He glanced up at the clock and sighed. His personal assistant would be going crazy wondering where he was. He was supposed to be doing interviews at the Ritz in less than an hour. He made a call and told them he would be unable to do any interviews; some took the news harder than others.

"What do you mean you can't come?" Martin, his director, barked down the phone. "You expect me to give this interview alone?"

"Matt and Sabrina will be attending as well. I have my PA team on hand to make all the arrangements and ensure everything goes to plan."

Martin grumbled something inaudible.

"Fine. But you're doing Tokyo next week," he snapped.

Harry took a breath. "No, I'm going to be busy for the rest of the month. Martin, I need you to take over this tour."

There was a silence. Then a deep sigh.

"I don't know what's going on with you but sounds serious if you're prepared to let the team down."

Ordinarily this would have made Harry change his mind; the thought of letting anyone down filled him with anguish. He would move mountains to make other people happy. But there someone more important he needed to please.

As if the universe was finally on his side, the door swung open and in strolled a man with the biggest arms Harry had ever seen. His face broke into a casual smirk, and he pulled his long hair into a man bun.

"Hey there, baby bro," his low voice boomed. "I heard you got yourself into a street fight."

Harry found himself grinning back.

"Jonas, I'm glad you're here," he said as they hugged. "I've got a huge favor to ask."

Jonas scratched his stubbly beard and cocked a brow at Harry with intrigue.

"I'm listening," he said, leaning against the wall. Harry stuffed his phone in his pocket and rested his hand on Jonas' shoulder. The hard muscle underneath flexed.

"I need you to teach me to be the alpha male."

Jonas clapped his hands and laughed.

"Oh, boy. This is going to be fun."

CHAPTER 23

Needles and Backbone

"Let me get this straight," Emily said, pacing Julie's living room. "You got attacked. Harry's in the hospital, and you've left him to be with the woman who engineered said attack who just happens to be his ex-fiancé?"

Julie's stomach tightened. When Emily put it that way, it sounded a lot less like an honorable sacrifice and a lot more like she left Harry to the wolves. Poor, sweet, kind Harry. The best man she'd ever met, and she left him to that... woman.

"We don't know the attack had anything to do with

Ebony," she reasoned, trying to assuage her guilt. Her suspicions were confirmed when minutes before the ambulance arrived, Ebony came running across the street. If she hadn't been involved, how did she know where they were?

"Oh, please," Emily said with an eye roll. "You don't think it's weird they jumped on Harry and left you alone?"

Julie crossed her legs and Tabby jumped into her lap.

"I defended myself."

"You defended Harry," Emily corrected. "You said they were only going for *him*."

Julie scratched Tabby's ears and listened to his deep purr. It was true, technically no one tried to throw any punches at Julie. Even when she fought them, they ran off rather than hit back. As ego-boosting as it was to believe she had scared off three men with her kick-boxing skills, it was too easy. Had Ebony told them to beat Harry up only?

"But if it was Ebony, why didn't she target me? It's me she wants out of the picture."

"Exactly," Emily said coming to a stop in the middle of the room and looking triumphant. As if she had just solved all of life's mysteries. "If she targeted you, it would only make Harry more determined to protect you. If it was the other way around, she knew you'd decide he was better off without you. Ebony knew you would break up with Harry."

Julie's head was spinning. Had she played perfectly into Ebony's hands?

"What else was I supposed to do?" She rubbed Tabby's belly making his paws twitch and eyes roll to the back of his head.

Emily sat on the couch beside Julie and tickled Tabby under his chin. The cat purred constantly, reveling in all of the attention.

"I'm just surprised you left so abruptly. Have you called Harry to see how he is?"

Julie looked away, unable to look at Emily's wide-eyed stare. They had an ability to see right through anyone, and she couldn't bring herself to tell her the truth. How could she contact him?

"Julie, you have to call him," Emily said firmly, reading her thoughts. "It's not fair on either of you to just break it off like this. You told me you were going to marry the man!"

Julie snapped her head back to Emily so fast her neck cracked.

"And say what? 'Hi Harry, how are you doing? So, I thought you and Ebony needed to figure some things out, so I'm giving you some space. If things are resolved and you're still interested in dating me, give me a call.' Yeah that would go down well."

"That's not bad actually," Emily said, looking thoughtful.

"Emily, I would sound like a heartless—"

"No you wouldn't. And it's the truth isn't it? If Ebony was no longer a problem, you would get back together, wouldn't you?"

"I don't know. Harry seems a bit too…"

"…much of a pushover?" Emily asked, her brows raised. Julie sighed. Emily was never afraid to say things bluntly. It was a quality she usually appreciated, but on this occasion the words stung. Yes, Harry didn't stand up for himself. It seemed like the people who worked for him owned him. And during the attack, he didn't even try to fight back. Ebony's words echoed in her mind like the bells of Notre Dame.

"When it comes to it, he won't fight for you."

Emily put her arm around Julie's shoulder and pulled her in for a hug.

"It's going to be okay. We'll figure this out," she said with a sigh as she patted Julie's hair. "You look exhausted. Go to bed and we'll catch up later."

Julie didn't need to be told twice. She trudged to bed and collapsed in a heap on top of her quilt. Her body had no idea what time zone she was in, and everything ached. She figured after some sleep she'd wake up with a clear head. But her dreams were invaded by nightmarish scenarios of exploding letters and death threats written in blood.

CHAPTER 24

WHO'S THE MAN?

"Give me thirty more."

Harry puffed as Jonas pressed his heel into his back with each push up. His biceps and shoulders were on fire, but he persisted.

"Come on, bro, don't quit now," Jonas shouted. Harry finished the final two and collapsed on the cold floor in a puddle of his own perspiration.

"Get up," Jonas ordered. Harry staggered to his feet and surveyed his reflection in the wall mirror. The outline of his muscles bulged, he looked pumped. His glistening six-pack was rock hard, giving Harry a sense of pride.

Jonas slapped a hand on his back and whistled. Harry's body was covered in faint bruises, and he ached in ways he never had before. But he didn't care. He needed to man up and fight for the love of his life.

"Now, go and make me a protein shake," Jonas barked. Harry looked at him with surprise before heading for the door, but Jonas thrust a hand in the way, the ripples of muscles along his arm were like mole hills.

"Wrong move. An alpha doesn't let anyone tell him what to do."

Harry stopped walking and scratched the back of his neck.

"Right," he said gruffly. "Make it yourself."

Jonas grinned, then walked across the gym to pick up a large rope. He flipped the end to snap at Harry's ankle like a whip. The contact sent pain radiating up his calf.

"What are you doing?" he said, hopping on one foot.

"Oh, sorry, did that hurt?" Jonas asked, though by the tone of his voice Harry thought he was not apologetic. He flipped the rope again. This time the end connected with Harry's thigh. A crack echoed around the gym and Harry yelled at the burning pain that followed.

"Cut it out, will you?" he said rubbing his thigh. A

large dimple formed on Jonas' right cheek as he flashed a smile.

"You don't like it?" he asked, rolling the rope back. "Want me to stop?" He whipped the rope again; this time Harry fell to his knees as he cried out.

"How is this helping?" he shouted, anger brewing. Jonas marched over to Harry and stooped down.

"I'm sorry, I thought you asked me to teach you to man up," he teased. "Now, if you want me to stop, you need to make me." He threw the rope across the room and flung it back in a snapping motion. Harry rolled out of its path and got to his feet.

"Stop doing that," he said, balling his hands into fists. Jonas squared up to Harry, raising his shoulders and grunting.

"Are you going to make me stop, or what?" he asked, shoving Harry, who stumbled back, then mirrored his brother's stance, squaring his shoulders and clenching his fists. The muscles in his arms were tight, begging for a reprieve. The two of them had been working day and night in the gym, training Harry to stand up for himself. He took a step forward and shoved his brother hard. However, the force barely made him move an inch. Instead, he stood his ground with a confident smirk on his tanned face.

"Why do they intimidate you so much?" Jonas asked suddenly.

Harry crossed his arms. "Who?"

"Mother and your ex. Why are you so afraid of their silly games?" Jonas rolled his shoulders back and cracked his knuckles. The sheer size of him was enough to scare off a whole group of bandits.

"I'm not scared for my sake. I am concerned about Julie."

"You want my advice?" Jonas asked. Harry nodded. Of course he wanted his advice. Jonas was the one who didn't take threats from anyone.

"Cut them both off. You've got the resources. Get some nice private place in Morocco and live your life in peace."

"Sounds nice, but I can't just hide away from the world. I need to stand my ground," Harry said resolutely.

"Then let's get some fight into you," he said, circling Harry now, looking thoughtful. "Talk to me about Julie."

Harry's ears pricked up. Just the sound of her name ignited a fire in his body. Jonas pulled on a pair of boxing gloves and threw a pair to Harry.

"Remind me, how did you two meet?" Jonas asked as Harry pulled on his gloves. Harry glanced at Benjamin, who stood at the door with his hands clasped together a vacant expression on his face.

"Through a mutual friend," he said. Sticking to the

same story he told every time Jonas asked. His brother raised his hands and the two of them boxed for a few minutes. Harry hadn't told anyone about hiring Emily to find him a girlfriend. Only Benjamin knew. If Jonas found out that he hired a matchmaker, he would never hear the end of it.

"And you still like her, I'm guessing," Jonas said, shaking his hands and hopping on tip toes.

"You could say that," Harry said as he panted.

"And you're sure you don't want to get back together with Ebony?" Jonas pulled off his gloves and folded his arms across his broad chest.

"No, definitely not."

Jonas nodded.

"Good. I never liked her anyway. I don't know why you wasted years in that relationship."

Harry sighed and picked up his flask from the floor.

"She's got some vendetta against me now. Our mother says it's love but sounds more like she's just looking for someone to torture."

"Why do you let her do it?" Jonas asked as Harry took a swig from his flask.

"Excuse me?" He spluttered as some of the drink went down the wrong way. "I'm not letting her do anything."

"So, your plan to stay in England for these past few weeks has not been torture for you?"

"*You've* been torturing me. Not her," Harry corrected. Jonas laughed as he stretched out his obliques.

"You're in denial, mate." He swung his arms back and forth and rolled his head side to side. "Staying away from Julie is killing you. I can see it all over your face."

Harry turned away and swallowed.

"I can't go back, not until I'm—"

"—a man? Please. You don't need to do this. You're ready."

Harry turned around to face his brother again, who gave him a frank smile that Harry couldn't read.

"What do you mean?"

Jonas dragged his hands through his hair and shook it out. Droplets of sweat scattered across the floor as he did so.

"You didn't come to me to get in shape. You and I both know that." Jonas scraped his damp hair back into a bun and set his hands on his hips like a superhero.

"Well, if you're too chicken to be with Julie, maybe I'll take her for a ride," Jonas said with a wry smile. Harry shot him a look.

"Steady," Harry warned. His muscles tensed again as adrenaline pumped through his veins. Jonas' eyes narrowed.

"You did say she was a good kisser. I bet she'd be amazing—"

Harry jumped to his feet, his hands balled into tight fists, his heart pounding against his ribcage.

"Don't talk about her like that," he spat at his brother, baring his teeth with a growl. Every atom in his body was on fire now. One more word and his fist would connect with Jonas' smug smile. He stared at him like a raging bull, eyeing a matador.

Jonas did a slow clap as he stood, then rested his hand on Harry's shoulder.

"You're ready," he said.

Harry stared at him as his pulse returned to normal and anger cooled.

"Benjamin," he shouted. "Get the car ready. We're going to the airport tonight."

CHAPTER 25

Finding Julie

Life without Harry Jackson was much less thrilling. Julie went back to her mundane routine. Sewing dresses by day, consuming far too much ice cream while watching soppy romances with Tabby by evening. Emily was busy matching rich people with their potential soul mate. And Julie's sense of purpose in life had dissipated.

She fell for Harry too fast. Some distance from him showed her that. At the same time, there was an old saying, "absence makes the heart grow fonder," and Julie saw the truth in that. Within days, they acted like eternal lovers. She became *that* girl, who she promised

LAURA BURTON

herself she'd never be. And it irritated her. But each
day that rolled by without seeing him or hearing his
voice seemed to create an even bigger hole in her
heart.

Julie was deciding which pair of leggings to pull on
when her phone vibrated on the bed. She bolted across
the room at lightning speed and took the call without
even looking at the screen.

"Hello?"

"Julie, it's Valentina Rose."

The silky voice on the other end of the phone
dulled her excitement a little, even after three weeks of
silence, she had hoped to hear Harry's voice.

"Valentina, how great to hear from you. How are
you doing?" Julie said in her fake, bright voice.

"I was hoping you would still consider designing a
dress for me? I know the Oscars isn't for a long time,
but I have this function at New York this weekend. I
know it's last minute, but I'd love to wear one of your
gowns."

Julie's heart accelerated in speed.

"Do you mean the Estelle Fashion Awards?" It was
the only big event she could think of that was
happening.

"Yes, that's it. I know you work for Estelle, so I
thought it would be a lovely fit."

Julie resisted the urge to squeal as she spun around on the spot, wondering what to say.

"How soon can you get here? I have a wardrobe filled with dresses to show you. We'll need to do some fittings and make alterations, as I'm sure they'll be too big. Oh yikes, we've got less than two days…."

"I am getting in a cab now. Send over your address. Is that too soon? I can find someone else to—"

"No, that's great. I'll send the details. Thank you so much Valentina, this is such an honor." Julie ended the call and did an excitable dance in her room as Tabby watched, lying on the bed.

"Tabby. Valentina Rose is going to be wearing one of *my* dresses to Estelle's Fashion Awards." Julie squealed and jumped up and down again as Tabby blinked lazily at her. Having a major Hollywood actress wearing one of her designs was the most exciting move in her career. There would be press and interviews. She'd be asked, "Who are you wearing?" and Valentina would reply, "Julie Andrews."

The thought made Julie want to run around her apartment screaming at the top of her lungs.

"Julie, I cannot thank you enough," Valentina gushed as Julie fastened the final pin in the yellow gown. The skirt fanned out at the knees and hugged every curve on Valentina's Latina body. The bright yellow material was a beautiful contrast to her deep skin tone; she looked like a walking sunset. Her long hair pulled back into a high ponytail.

"You look divine, darling," Frederick, her stylist said as he finished touching up her makeup. Julie stood in the Marks Hotel, marveling at all the marble and granite surfaces. The dressing room had mirrors surrounding a small foot stool perched on a center island, offering Valentina a look at herself in every angle. There were five stylists, a hair dresser, PA, and bodyguard in the room. Julie had no idea how many people were involved when it came to getting ready for a big event. Valentina looked like a golden goddess. She glided across the room with so much elegance, Julie wondered if she was hiding a hoverboard under her dress.

The Estelle Fashion Awards was an annual event that attracted designers from all across the globe to show off their new lines. Valentina got VIP passes for Julie, who made no hesitation in handing the other one to Emily.

. . .

Julie walked into the events hall and peered through all of the faces. An arm waved above the crowd and Julie stood on tiptoes to catch a glimpse of Emily's beaming face from the back of the room. A runway and stage was set, taking up a huge part of the room. Julie sidled past the rows of guests as she waded her way to join Emily.

"This. Is. Amazing," Emily said with a little squeal. Her dark hair was gelled back and she looked like she gone over-the-top with her body glitter. Every inch of her exposed décolletage was sparkly.

The show consisted of a lot of clapping, models walking up and down the cat walk, and Emily's commentary of how much fun she was having. Julie soon suffered with a headache, as their seats were right next to one of the large speakers. The booming music seemed to beat against her eardrums and when the show ended, she was excited to leave.

"No, we can't leave now," Emily burst out as Julie tried to make break for the exit. "You need to talk to these people. You know, network." She pushed Julie's back and steered her toward a group of designers who appeared to be deep in conversation.

"Emily, no," Julie hissed back over her shoulder as she flashed a sheepish smile at the designers and sidestepped to avoid breaking into their circle. "I want to go home. My head is killing me."

"You're not still pining over Harry, are you? Julie, this is your moment. Make the most of it!" Emily gestured to the crowd of talking people as if they were fish in the ocean, primed and ready to be collected.

"You stay. I know you love this sort of thing. But I'm going to get a cab," Julie said holding Emily's shoulders. "Thank you for coming with me."

"Are you sure?" Emily asked, chewing her lip. Julie rubbed her arm and gave her a reassuring smile.

"Completely. Enjoy yourself and tell me everything in the morning, okay? I'll have cinnamon rolls fresh out of the oven."

"Promise?" Emily asked, her face breaking into a grin.

The two of them hugged and said their good-byes as Julie waded through the crowd of people. Now the award ceremony was over, everyone stood filling all the space in the room.

"Ms. Andrews, I do not remember seeing your name on the guest list." Frank's voice sent a shiver down Julie's spine as he came into view. He stood looking austere in a sharp pinstripe suit, a drink in hand and his nose scrunched as if he was offended by a bad smell.

"I was added last minute," Julie said curtly. Her

fingers curled into the palms of her hands as she fought to keep her breathing steady.

I will not let this idiot ruin my night.

"Estelle would never have allowed that. Only designers are allowed seats at this even, not simple dressmakers." His eyes squinted as he offered a false smile and took a sip of his drink. Julie straightened her back and held her head high.

"I am a designer. Valentina Rose is wearing one of my dresses, and after tonight I won't need to endure you and your insufferable peppermint breath again."

Frank's mouth fell open as his face paled and his hand flew to cover his breath.

"Excuse me—"

Julie held up a hand to him in silence and walked away. A beaming smile creeping across her face.

She fought her way to the back door and pushed it open to be greeted with the cool New York evening air whipping through her hair. Julie's heart was racing. Finally, she stood up to Frank and put him in his place. She knew she would likely have no job tomorrow, but she didn't care.

Julie sighed and took in the familiar sounds of the city. Honking horns, the constant stream of traffic, and people in the street talking loudly. Underneath the dark sky, Julie felt safe. In the dark, she was under the radar.

And as she rounded the corner and walked away from Estelle's tower, the sounds grew quieter.

Harry's face entered Julie's mind once more. She wanted to pick up the phone and call him with the news that Valentina Rose was wearing her gown to the Estelle Fashion Awards. Whatever happened next in her career, she knew one thing, she was not just a seamstress. Now she could market herself as a designer. A designer who made gowns for A-list celebrities.

Okay, celebrity. But this is just the beginning.

The achievement felt hollow somehow. Her excitement dulled by the constant ache in her heart. All she wanted to do was pick up the phone and call Harry. It had been weeks and he hadn't sent her so much as a text. Complete radio silence. It was maddening. However, she was the one who'd made the decision to leave. Her mind replayed the events on repeat. There was no other way to keep Harry safe. He must have known that too, or else he would have reached out to her, surely?

She wasn't happy. Even after the biggest moment in her career, Julie realized that without someone to share it with, her life would never be anything other than average. Maybe there was a way they could be together. They never had the opportunity to go over their options. Harry had money. Lots of it. Surely, they could work something out. Was she willing to let a jealous redhead limit her happiness—even if she was crazy and most definitely dangerous?

Julie wasn't sure if it was the ego boost from the evening, or the sudden epiphany that seemed to spark in her mind that had her so pumped full of adrenaline, but she walked mindlessly along the road, head held high and a drunken smile plastered on her face. She did not notice the quiet road she had stumbled upon, nor the lone black car parked innocently beside a dumpster. Her only thoughts were seeing Harry's face lighting up and his arms wrapping around her body, when something suddenly struck the back of her head.

As if by slow motion, Julie fell forward, startled and her ears ringing. Hands caught her body and someone thrust a scratchy sack over her head. Julie's brain froze. As if it had lost signal to her limbs, she fell limp as multiple hands secured her legs and arms and carried her forward. She thought it would be a good idea to scream, but her headache was a full-on migraine now after the hit, and would anyone hear her with a sack over her head? So she lay still, and didn't fight back.

Emily's words played in her mind. Had it been her fighting back that helped Harry in London, or had it all been a ruse and she really had no power to fight and defend herself?

Julie's shoulders banged a carpeted floor and someone tucked her legs up by her chin her gown ripped at the seam up to her thigh. A rumble under-neath her told her she was in the back of a vehicle. Something slammed above her head, then, she heard muffled talking.

Julie kept her breathing steady as she berated herself for not being more streetwise. She was on her way to her imminent demise, and there was nothing anyone could do about it.

CHAPTER 26

THE WOLF AND THE LAMB

arry spotted Emily in the crowd of well-dressed guests. He adjusted his tie nervously as he made his way through the people and waved to her. She glanced at him and finished her conversation with a bright smile before turning toward Harry with a look to kill.

"What are you doing here?" she asked, her eyes narrowed, and lips pressed tightly together.

"I'm looking for Julie," he said, scanning the room for her familiar form.

"Oh, and what about Ebony?" Emily asked, crossing her arms with an unimpressed look.

"What about her? I've told her we're not getting back together. She won't be a problem," he said. Emily gave him a look that said she wasn't convinced. But there was no time. Now he was here, he needed to see Julie. To hold her hand and look into her amber-colored eyes. Tell her he loved her.

"You've just missed her. She left to call a cab a few minutes ago."

Harry nodded and made to leave but Emily grabbed his arm; he tensed and surveyed the intense expression on her face.

"She's my best friend, you know. If you hurt her again, I will kill you."

"She's lucky to have you," he replied. Emily's resolve broke as her lips curved upward.

Without another moment wasted, Harry rushed through the crowd of people and ran out onto the street. A line of cabs sat by the side of the road. He jogged alongside them peering in through the windows to catch a glimpse of Julie. At the corner of the street he looked left and right, but she was nowhere to be seen.

"Sir, do you think this is a good idea?" Benjamin said, catching up to him.

"We can work through this. I can feel it. Besides, nothing is going to stop me trying. I love her, Benjamin. What else can I do?"

His phone vibrated and he pulled it out of his pocket.

"Benjamin…" He lost his voice. A picture loaded on the screen of a woman tied up, wearing a purple gown with a brown sack over her head. He showed the phone to Benjamin, who took it out of his hands.

"See that graffiti on the wall? I know where that is," he said. "Come on." He gestured for Thomas, who opened the car door and the two of them climbed in. Harry's hands were trembling and a tightness spread across his chest. He pulled out his inhaler and took a deep breath.

He didn't listen to Benjamin giving Thomas directions, nor did he pay attention to the nausea rising from the pit of his stomach. He just stared at the image on his phone, with four accompanying words.

She dies at midnight.

This was it. No turning back now. Julie was in danger, and it was up to him to save her. No matter the cost.

The car pulled up alongside the Brooklyn Bridge.

"Down here," Benjamin said, as they stumbled down the slippery path. The area was entirely deserted. It was the perfect place to take a hostage—only sewer rats came this far down to the drains. They rounded the corner and Harry saw two men standing next to a woman lying on the ground. Harry, pulled off his jacket and rolled his sleeves up. The men had black ski masks covering their faces, but there was no doubt who they were and what they wanted.

"What's your price?" he asked. The woman twitched and made a muffled cry.

"One million. Each," one of the masked captors said. He raised a gun to Harry, his finger on the trigger.

"Done. Now release her," Harry said. The two men laughed.

"Not so fast, we want the money first."

Harry dragged a hand through his hair.

"I don't think you understand; I can't just do an online transfer for that amount of money. I'd need to go into a bank."

"*You* don't understand. She dies at midnight if you don't bring us the money."

Harry grit his teeth. Jonas' grin flashed across his mind's eye. He wouldn't stand for this. Whoever these people were, they knew Harry would roll over and do whatever they wanted. But who was to say they wouldn't pull this stunt again next time they want more money? This needed to end. Harry took a step forward. The two men flinched. Both of them held a gun pointed at him now.

"Easy," one of them warned, as Harry took another step.

"That's close enough," the other one said. Harry clenched his fists and blinked at the sight of the two masked men. The sound of his voice was unsure. He could hear his fear.

"Take that bag off her head. We can be more civilized that this." Harry was less than two feet away from the men now. He watched one of the men hesitantly pull the sack and drop it on the wet cement. Julie's blotchy face came into view; her platinum hair fanned across her cheeks and she blinked at him, adjusting her eyes to the streetlight.

"Are you all right?"

Julie stared at him, blinking, as if she was in shock or deciding whether this was a nightmare. She finally gave a nod. Harry turned to the men. One of them was watching Julie, while the other remained focused on Harry. He was close enough now that in one sweeping motion, he could disarm one man. The problem was, he wasn't sure if he could be fast enough to deal with the other guy before Julie got hurt.

"The banks are closed, so we'll need to arrange this in the morning. Now I suggest we go back to my apartment—"

"We're not stupid," the first man snapped. "You'll have the cops on us in a heartbeat. I'm telling you, if you don't give us this money by midnight, she'll die."

"Don't do it, Harry. They'll just kill me anyway,"

Julie said in a resolved tone. There was no sign of fear in *her* voice. Then everything happened in a flash. The second man threw his leg back to kick Julie, but she must have broken out of the ties. She was suddenly in a crouch position and grabbed his leg pushing it back so hard he tripped and fell back. In the commotion, Harry grabbed the gun from the first man and head-butted him with the handle.

A loud crack echoed under the bridge and the man screeched with pain. Harry grabbed the gun from the first man and head-butted him with the back of it.

"Benjamin, call the police," Harry shouted as Julie kicked the second man behind the knees, ensuring he stayed on the ground. Harry stood above the men, holding the gun trained on them, then looked at Julie's determined face and bit his lip to stop himself from grinning. Adrenaline pulsing through his body, making all of his senses sharper.

"Benjamin, did you—" A click caught his attention and Julie and Harry looked up to see Benjamin standing a few feet away with a gun pointed directly at Harry.

"What the—" Then, as if he and Julie had been struck by the same thought they bent down and removed the ski-masks from Julie's captors.

"No," Harry moaned. Looking at the two faces.

Two men from his security team. Benjamin's sinister laugh chilled Harry to the bone.

"It was you? All along?" he said faintly. Benjamin raised his free hand.

"Guilty," he said blankly.

"But why?"

Benjamin scratched his chin.

"It was supposed to be simple. You and Ebony would get back together, and then I'd get a nice reward to let me retire early."

"Money? So my mother was paying you to do this?"

"If I remember correctly, your mother said, 'break them apart at all costs.' She was quite upset when the boys beat you up, though, so that was taking it too far apparently, but it seemed like our plan worked. You were in London. She was here. Neither of you were speaking. Soon enough, you'd end up with Ebony and I would get my payout."

Benjamin took a few steps forward and gave a heavy sigh.

"But then you had to go and have a change of heart. Realizing that life wasn't worth living without Julie. I had to endure your laughable sessions with your brother. Who do you think you are, Rocky?" He rolled his eyes. "Trust me, if you hand over the money, all of this will go away." He waved a hand aside to cement his point, then he glared at Harry. "But if you don't pay up...." He moved the gun to direct it at Julie.

A bolt of energy shot through Harry's body like someone injected pure adrenaline straight to his heart. It was as if he saw red and nothing else mattered. Seeing Benjamin threaten Julie sent pure rage flooding through his senses. This was it. The moment he had been training for. Benjamin, his most trusted body guard. A traitor. Hired by his own mother. Now threatening to hurt the love of his life.

Not on my watch.

Harry released the safety on the gun in his hand and fired. Benjamin's knee gave way and he dropped his gun to the ground with a howl. Julie quickly grabbed it and held it trained on the men. Harry walked over to Benjamin who was yelping like a wounded puppy as he cradled his knee.

"You shot me," he shouted. "You weren't supposed to shoot me."

Harry crouched down and muttered into Benjamin's ear. "You weren't supposed to betray me, but look where we are."

Benjamin's breaths came out rapid and shallow as he raised his hands in the air. "I swear. None of this was part of the plan," he said between breaths. Harry lowered the gun a little and gave him a hard look.

"Tell me then, what was the plan? And who told

you to do this?" he said, surveying every inch of Benjamin's pale and clammy face, daring him to lie.

"Okay. Okay," he said, lowering his hands and wincing as he cradled his knee again. "It was supposed to be a simple job. For a long time now, your stepfather has been paying us to feed information back to your mother."

Harry shook his head in disbelief.

There never was a private investigator.

His mother had his own security team spy on him. The thought made him sick to his stomach.

"When you met Julie, I was ordered to put you off pursuing her."

"There wasn't a kid who slashed the tires, was there?"

Benjamin shook his head with his eyes shut.

"And the thugs in London? That was you?"

Benjamin opened his eyes and giant tear leaked out and rolled down his cheek. Harry couldn't be sure if he was crying with regret over his actions or over the gunshot wound.

"Your mother was angry about that. Told us we took a step too far and the deal was off. Problem is, I had people waiting for that money. A gambling debt that I couldn't run away from, and I was desperate."

"So how was all this supposed to work out?" Julie asked, taking a step forward. Harry glanced up to see her dress soaked with dark stains and the seam had been torn.

"Since I wasn't going to get the money from his parents for breaking you too up, I needed Harry to pay the money. I would have handed in my resignation leaving you two in peace. It was the honorable thing to do, at least," Benjamin said with a sigh.

"What do you know about honorable?" Harry shot back. He laughed derisively and looked away as he processed the information. "Gambling debt? So this really was all about money for you?"

"You'll be surprised what people do when they're desperate," Benjamin said as he shifted his weight and moaned. "When your mother ended the deal after my guys took it too far, I had no other choice."

Harry was torn. Part of him wanted to kick Benjamin in the knee, but the other part of him pitied him. He couldn't imagine being so desperate for money that he would do *anything* to get it. He was relieved to know his mother was more innocent in this than he had thought. It was a bit of a surprise, however. Ebony was not behind the threats, after all

He opened his mouth to talk but Julie spoke first.

"Harry, not here. Can't you see how much he's bleeding? We need to call the police and get an ambulance to take him to hospital," Julie said, quickly. Harry stared at Benjamin as Julie tugged at his jacket.

"Harry, come on," Julie urged. Forcing Harry to his feet.

He turned to Julie, as if seeing her for the very first time. He cradled her cheek and smoothed his thumb across her clammy skin.

"I've missed you," he said shakily. Her eyes were like two balls of fire, warming his heart. There were so many unanswered questions and he wasn't quite sure if he was about to wake up at any moment. But he knew one thing. "I love you," he said before planting a kiss on her lips. Julie laughed against his mouth and broke away, still attempting to hold the gun on the two men on the ground.

"Is now really the time?" she asked.

Harry opened his mouth to speak when a loud bang almost exploded his eardrums and knocked the wind out of him. Julie's smile faded and the look of horror covered her face as Harry fell to his knees.

"Harry!" Her scream sounded far away and muffled, as if he was floating in water. An unearthly siren filled the air and there were more bangs. Harry fell down, his cheek pressed against the cold, damp cement, and he tasted blood in his mouth.

Harry blinked slowly as his body became numb and heavy.

"No, please, don't leave me."

Never.

CHAPTER 27

CONSPIRACY THEORIES

J ulie took a shaking hand to her face and stared at the blood drenching her index finger. Harry's blood. She looked over and was shocked to see Benjamin dead on the ground with his eyes still open.

"Are you all right ma'am?" a police officer approached her as another handcuffed the two men who'd remained silent. They did not even try to fight or argue against their arrest.

"We need an ambulance," she said to the officer as he inspected Harry. He gave a nod and pressed his gloved hand on Harry's back.

"We need to keep pressure on the wound. Hold on, there's a first aid kit in the car. Put your hand here—" He lifted his and Julie pressed down, stemming the blood flow. The officer jogged back up the pass to his car. The lights flashed red and blue, illuminating the entire area. Julie felt Harry's pulse through her hands.

"Stay alive. Just please, stay alive," she said.

"Julie, oh thank goodness. Julie are you okay?"

Julie looked up to see Emily running to them while holding her skirt up.

"Emily, what are you doing here? How did you—"

Emily held up her phone.

"After what happened to you in London, I wanted to keep an eye on you. Our friends app shows me your location. When Harry ran after you and I saw you were here, I knew something was wrong. Thankfully, I persuaded these guys to drive me over." She gestured to the police car.

"Are you all right?" she repeated, kneeling down beside her and placing a hand on her back. Julie nodded but her arms were shaking. She was nauseated and light-headed.

"He's been shot. It's bad, Emily."

Emily nodded slowly with saucer-like eyes.

"Help is on the way. He'll be okay," she said in a weak voice. Julie was not convinced.

"We won. We had them, Emily. Then there was a

gunshot and Harry just fell." She broke off and closed her eyes. Tears rolled down her face leaving a burning trail over her cheeks. When Harry collapsed, Julie saw Benjamin on the ground with a gun in hand. He must have had another one on him that he'd pulled out when Harry had his back turned. Then in a flash, there were more gunshots and Benjamin was dead.

The next few hours passed by in a blur of questions, camera flashes, sirens, and Emily's non-stop talking. She rubbed Julie's back, handed her a bottle of water, held her hand, and guided her to the waiting room at the hospital. Then, in her anxious state of mind, talked endlessly.

"Let me get this straight, Benjamin was paid to spy on Harry." She started to pace the waiting room as Julie clutched the cup of hot chocolate in her hand and stared at the floor.

"And all the threats, that fake goat display—" Emily gasped as Julie nodded along.

"Yes. When we saw it, Benjamin got his men to take the sign down and when Harry asked him about informing the police and fingerprints he just dismissed it and told us he would handle it and just needed to get us to safety. Wow, it's all starting to make sense now."

"You've got to hand it to them for imagination." Emily noted.

Julie shot her a look. "Really?"

Emily's face fell as if she realized the seriousness of the situation, then began to pace again.

"So… Ebony is innocent in all of this? She didn't hire people to beat Harry up?"

"Yes, but she knew what Harry's mother was doing. I wouldn't exactly call her innocent." Julie took a sip of the hot chocolate and sighed as the sugary fluid calmed her nerves.

"But why would Benjamin turn on Harry like that? He's got money too, probably pays him far more than he should, and he's so likeable. I don't get it."

Before Julie could think of a reply, a bustle of movement in the corner of her eye caught her attention. Mrs. Bowood entered the hospital and hurried over to the reception desk.

"I got on a plane as soon as I heard—" she said in a breathy voice then turned to see Julie. "Heard anything yet?" Julie shook her head. Mrs. Bowood's face wrinkled as she broke down.

"How did you know?" Julie blurted out. Benjamin was dead, his cronies were sitting in a cell, and Harry had been in surgery for the last six hours.

Just how many spies does this woman have?

"Heavens' sake. You're all over the news," Mrs. Bowood said wiping her eyes. She walked over to Julie and held out her hand. It was a white flag. But Julie was not sure she was ready to accept it.

"I never wanted any of this to happen," Mrs. Bowood said.

"I know," Julie said frankly. "Benjamin confessed. We know everything." She rose to her feet and Mrs. Bowood glanced at Emily who had her hands on her hips.

"I was going to tell Harry the truth. All of it. I even called Benjamin last night when Harry left...." Her voice faded away as she looked from Julie to Emily lost for words. Emily folded her arms, she remained silent but the look of thunder on her face showed that she was resisting the urge to rant.

Julie bit her lip against her own outburst. How could a mother be so manipulative? Julie's face must have given her thoughts away though, because Mrs. Bowood raised her brows at her.

"You're not a mother," she said her voice rising in pitch. "I had to have someone watch Harry. For his own good."

J ulie sat and rolled her head side to side with a yawn. Her muscles were seizing up. They had been at the hospital so long that morning light was starting to peer in through the windows.

"I don't care. None of this matters right now. I just

need to know he's okay," she said tiredly. Emily sat in the chair beside Julie and took her hand.

"He's going to be okay. I can feel it," she muttered.

Mrs. Bowood dragged her hand over her face and sighed.

"I'm going to make a call," she said heavily and marched back through the doors to the parking lot.

Julie scowled at the floor. Kicking herself.

"I can't believe I didn't *do* anything," She replayed the moment she was captured. She couldn't believe how her body and mind had betrayed her. Why did she allow herself to become distracted in that alley. If she had just kept alert, and then fought like she'd been taught, then maybe....

"Don't beat yourself up, you know that none of this is your fault," Emily said firmly while squeezing her hand.

Before Julie could argue, the doors swung open and a surgeon entered the waiting room. Julie and Emily jumped to their feet as they crossed the room.

"You are Harold's girlfriend, right?" Julie nodded. Girlfriend sounded so small and simple. Soul mate. Eternal love. Partner in crime. Any of those would have been better than girlfriend.

"The surgery was a success. I was able to remove the bullet and control the bleeding. Thankfully, his vital organs weren't hit. He's very lucky."

"He's going to live?" Julie asked, hardly daring to breathe.

"He is stable. I'm going to keep him in for a few days to monitor, and he'll be on prophylactic antibiotics to guard against infection."

"Can I see him?" Julie clung onto Emily's hand for dear life.

The woman nodded. "A nurse will be out to take you to him."

"Thank you so much, I don't know what to say."

"You're welcome." She smiled, then walked to the reception desk and spoke to the nurses as Julie waited with bated breath.

"Julie Andrews? Follow me. I'll take you to see Mr. Jackson," a short brunette said with oversized glasses. She brushed crumbs from her scrubs and walked to the double doors.

"I'll wait here and tell his mother the news," Emily said softly, giving Julie's hand one last squeeze before she let go. Julie gave her a brave smile before she took a deep breath, smoothed down her hair and followed the nurse.

The white sterile corridor with its blinding lights had a numbing effect on Julie. As she focused on placing one foot in front of another, a rising sense of panic crept up her arms. She could no longer feel her hands. Her elbows tingled and a heaviness sat on her chest that she couldn't shake. The nurse stopped and opened a door. As she stepped aside, Julie peered in to see Harry laying in a hospital bed. She entered the room and noted this was the second time she had come to visit Harry in hospital. *Although this time*, she promised herself as she brushed his hair away from his forehead with her fingertips, *I won't run away.*

Mrs. Bowood did not come into the room and Harry was in and out as he recovered from the surgery, leaving Julie to her thoughts.

The last twenty-four hours had been a whirlwind. She was finally recognized as a designer, stood up to Frank, then got kidnapped all in one night. Benjamin was dead and Harry had been shot. Now Mrs. Bowood was in town. The situation sent her mind spinning. Did Mrs. Bowood know about Benjamin's gambling problem? Did she not guess he would go to such lengths for money when she called off the deal? She sat beside the bed lost in various scenarios for hours when Harry stirred. His brows were tightly knitted together and he pouted his lips. Julie pressed her lips against his forehead.

His eyes blinked open and zoomed around the room before settling on Julie. Then a weak smile took over his frown.

"Well, aren't you a sight for sore eyes," he said faintly. Julie perched herself on the edge of the bed and stroked his face, tears falling freely as the bubble of emotion burst and came flooding out.

"I thought I lost you," she said between sobs. Harry patted her leg gently and shushed her.

"You never lost me. I'm fine, see? Barely even a scratch."

Julie wiped her eyes furiously. "Three weeks, Harry. Three weeks you didn't even text."

"Neither did you. And you ran off...."

Julie sighed as she studied the hurt on Harry's face.

"Why did you come back?" she asked weakly. Harry grazed his thumb across her cheek and the corners of his eyes creased as he looked at her lovingly.

"Because I needed to tell you that I love you."

The words flowed through her senses as if she had just jumped into a pool of warm honey. The panic calmed and her defenses melted away. All of her worries evaporated, they no longer mattered. All she cared about was that Harry loved her.

"I love you too," she said leaning in.

The two of them shared a tender kiss. Julie's lashes brushed against Harry's cheek and for a fleeting moment, she even forgot they were in hospital.

"And I know this isn't the perfect place to do this, but I can't wait any longer. Will you consider being my wife?"

Julie froze. In her mind, they were back in Lincoln

Center, with the beautiful orchestra playing, and Harry was at her feet dressed in a dark suit. This time, Julie did not give an off-the-cuff response, neither did she laugh. She placed both of her hands on his cheeks and looked him square in the eye.

"Yes. With all my heart. Yes."

They kissed again, a little too roughly because one of the machines started beeping. The noise jolted Julie out of her blissful state of mind and alerted her to the situation.

"Your mother is here. What do you want to do about her?" she said as she broke away. "I spoke to the police. They want to question everyone. Ebony too. It sounds like they're building a case on those two guys who captured me, I'm sure they'd be willing to testify if they get a deal."

Harry pressed his finger to Julie's lips and she stopped talking.

"We'll figure it out. I promise," he said in a hushed voice. Julie exhaled shakily. Just talking about it all was getting her worked up again. "Come here." He pulled her down and the two of them kissed again, Julie was careful to avoid the wires on his chest this time. They were interrupted by a vibration on the bed. Julie looked down.

"Do you need to take that?" she asked, holding out the phone to him. Harry took the phone and threw it across the room. Julie jumped with a gasp as it clattered to the floor and after a few moments fell silent. Then she looked back at Harry in shock as he grinned at her.

"Now, where were we?" he asked and Julie, matching his grin, leaned down once more.

The End.

EPILOGUE

EDWARD MARKS

Edward Marks sat swirling his drink in his hand as he listened to the maid of honor give her speech.

"The first day my best friend Julie met Harry, I remember saying to her, 'It's a beautiful day to fall in love,' and little did I know, that these two lovebirds would do exactly that." The room laughed. "I knew they were perfect for each other—being a matchmaker gives me a super power of sorts. But I didn't expect it to happen so fast."

"David, pour us another will you," Edward murmured to his brother who obliged. He looked at Julie, sitting next to her new husband, their faces were glowing with happiness. A twinge of jealousy tugged at his stomach. Harold Jackson was the awkward kid at school. He told jokes that people groaned at, never stood up for himself, and *he* got married first.

Not that Edward was willing to settle down anytime soon.

"Hey, did you hear that?" Sam nudged his arm and pointed to the stand. "She loved him for who he was. I bet you couldn't get a girl to fall in love with you if she didn't know you were a billionaire."

"Yeah, right. Ladies fall for my charm, not my wallet."

Sam chortled as he reclined in the back of his chair.

"Keep telling yourself that, mate."

"No, you haven't seen my game. I could be a dry cleaner and women would fall at my feet."

"That's just it. Always a game with you isn't it?" Howard said with a sigh. The corners of his eyes drooped downward, making him look constantly bored.

Edward sat up and looked between the gentleman, affronted. He turned to his brother. "David, back me up here," he said.

David rubbed his neck and inhaled deeply.

"I don't know what to say. You do like to flash the cash around women," he said.

Edward resisted the urge to roll his eyes.

Well, you're no help.

"How, I ask you, do I *flash the cash?*"

"Remember when you bought a yacht and named it after that girl you met at the theatre?"

"Or what about the time he organized a private concert with Beyoncé just because Halle—was it? told you she was a fan?"

"Don't forget that girl in Morocco."

Edward raised his hands in defeat.

"All right, all right. But I'm telling you. I don't need money to woo a woman. I've got skills," he said offering his most charming smile.

"You want to bet on that?" Sam asked with a wry smile. Howard made a noise of excitement and his droopy eyes lit up for the first time.

"Now this just got rather interesting," he said stroking his dark beard.

"Edward, come on. You don't do bets," David said in a low voice. Edward rolled his shoulders back and downed the rest of his drink.

"Call it a challenge, then. All right, Sam. I'm listening," he said as the string quartet started to play Mozart. Sam clapped and shifted in his seat with a grin.

"I challenge you to find a woman—who doesn't know you're filthy rich—and get her to fall in love with you within ten days."

Edward shrugged.

"Piece of cake," he said cracking his neck. Sam held up a stubby finger and shook his head.

"That's not all, my friend. You can't use more than a thousand dollars."

"Per date?" Edward asked, shocked. Sam threw his head back and laughed.

"In total. From the time you first meet, to the moment she says 'I love you' and seals it with a kiss."

"I never knew you were so romantic, Sam," David said patting his shoulder. Edward swallowed as he looked at Sam. All eyes were on him now as he considered it.

"What's the prize if I win?"

"Are you kidding? True love and a woman who is crazy enough to love you without any of the benefits," Sam said. The men chuckled.

"And if I lose?"

Sam looked thoughtful and rubbed his arm. Then a massive smile spread across his whole face.

"You give me your penthouse in New York... and you lose bragging rights. Plus, you'll know that a woman will never love you without money."

Ouch.

Edward looked up to see Harold taking Julie by the hand as the two of them took to the dance floor. Her huge dress took up so much space there was barely any room for other people to dance. Not that the couple noticed. Harold's eyes were only on Julie as they shared identical smiles, circling on the spot. He turned back at Sam's expectant face and held out his hand.

"Get a woman to fall in love with me within ten days."

Sam inclined his head.

"And spend no more than a thousand dollars in the process," he added firmly.

Edward nodded as they shook on it.

"Deal."

—Read Edward's story in Who Wants to Kiss a Billionaire? Here: mybook.to/kissabillionaire

Made in the USA
Columbia, SC
19 March 2021